THE … TON!

"A pure charmer, a rich Southern tale about love and loyalty."

—*Bookpage*

"As cozy as a cup of tea and a favorite cat, the latest in the Covington series will delight fans. . . . Fans of Jan Karon and Ann Ross will enjoy these gentle novels."

—*Booklist*

"A must-read for women of all ages."

—*The Tampa Tribune*

"Genuinely inspiring. . . . The reader can't help but be moved by the 'ladies' and their progress."

—*Library Journal*

"Ms. Medlicott is attuned to the nuances of Southern life and draws her characters with affectionate understanding, and an inspiring message of self-acceptance, courage, and survival."

—*The Dallas Morning News*

"A winner. . . . The three ladies inspire by forming a community in which they thrive and find new careers and loves, all with dignity and autonomy."

—*Publishers Weekly*

"A heartwarming adventure."

—*San Jose Mercury News*

"There's never a dull moment."

—*Atlanta Journal-Constitution*

"Medlicott captures small town life and . . . presents a charming story."

—*Chatanooga Times/Free Press*

"[A] charming story of small-town life. Wholesome and appealing."

—*Booklist*

"I have always enjoyed Joan Medlicott's books. The characters stay with you long after you finish."

—Jude Deveraux

"Settle back in a comfortable chair and enjoy your visit to Covington, a town rich with charm and character."

—*New York Times* bestselling author Debbie Macomber

"The ladies of Covington sow seeds of courage and community that bloom throughout this small mountain town and deep into the heart of every reader."

—Lynne Hinton, author of *Friendship Cake*

"The issues . . . are as fresh as tomorrow's news. Medlicott's prose is warm and quick. These three women, in their widow's might, inspire us with dignity and confidence, humor and affection."

—Robert Morgan, author of *Gap Creek*

"Proof that a woman's life begins, not ends, at a certain age, that men are nice to have around, but women friends are indispensable. A satisfying, warmhearted look at friendship that endures."

—Sandra Dallas, author of *Alice's Tulips*

"Her characters are so real that I began to miss them as soon as I closed the book. *From the Heart of Covington* is a book that is inspiring an easy to love, one that shows us the true meaning of friendship, family ties, and grace."

—Silas House, author of *Clay's Quilt*

"What a pleasure it is to meet the ladies of Covington once again. Their courage, humor, and wisdom, and their sensible, loving regard for the seasons of life and of nature, are gifts for us all."

—Nancy Thayer, author of *The Hot Flash Club*

"Come sit on the porch for a while with three unforgettable women. Bravo, ladies of Covington, I love you all!"

—Rosemary Rogers, author of *A Reckless Encounter*

ALSO BY JOAN MEDLICOTT

The Ladies of Covington Send Their Love
The Gardens of Covington
From the Heart of Covington
The Spirit of Covington
At Home in Covington
The Three Mrs. Parkers
A Covington Christmas
Two Days After the Wedding

JOAN MEDLICOTT

An Unexpected Family

POCKET BOOKS
NEW YORK LONDON TORONTO SYDNEY

POCKET BOOKS, a division of Simon & Schuster, Inc.
1230 Avenue of the Americas, New York, NY 10020

Library of Congress Cataloging-in-Publication Data

Medlicott, Joan A. (Joan Avna)
An unexpected family / Joan Medlicott
p. cm.
ISBN-13: 978-1-4165-2456-4
ISBN-10: 1-4165-2456-8
1. Older women—Fiction. 2. Female friendship—Fiction. 3. North Carolina. 4. Boardinghouses—Fiction. 5. Retired women—Fiction. I Title.

PS3563.E246U54 2007
813'.54—dc22

2006053281

This Pocket Books trade paperback edition April 2007

10 9 8 7 6 5 4 3

Manufactured in the United States of America

For information regarding special discounts for bulk purchases, please contact Simon & Schuster Special Sales at 1-800-456-6798 or business@simonandschuster.com.

Acknowledgments

Heartfelt thanks to Members of the Depot Committee:

Retha Ward, Forrest Jarrett, Lewis Eugene Wild, and Everett Boone for their generosity and warmth, for the wonderful tour, and for sharing the history of the building from its origin as a train depot through renovations that have made the Depot in Marshall, NC, the popular dance hall and music center it has become.

My thanks to Joan Bannister of Lancashire, England, for the songs that Sadie sang at the river and in the car in South Carolina.

To Anna Dehlia Delgado Miller,
my unexpected family, my sister

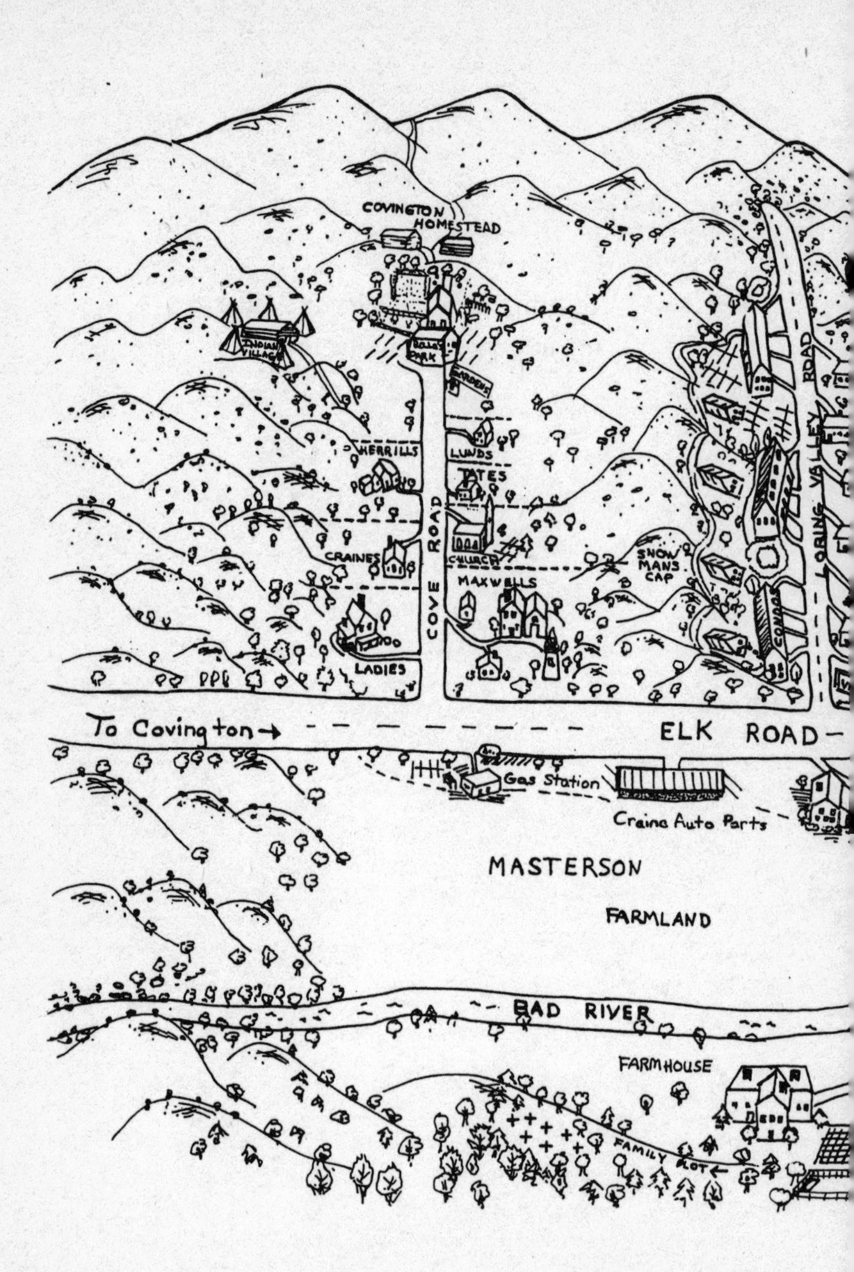

COVINGTON HOMESTEAD
INDIAN VILLAGE
PARK
GARDENS
HERRILLS
LUNDS
TATES
CHURCH
CRAINES
MAXWELLS
LADIES
COVE ROAD
SNOW MANS CAP
CONDOS
LORING VALLEY ROAD
To Covington →
ELK ROAD
Gas Station
Craine Auto Parts
MASTERSON
FARMLAND
BAD RIVER
FARMHOUSE
FAMILY PLOT ←

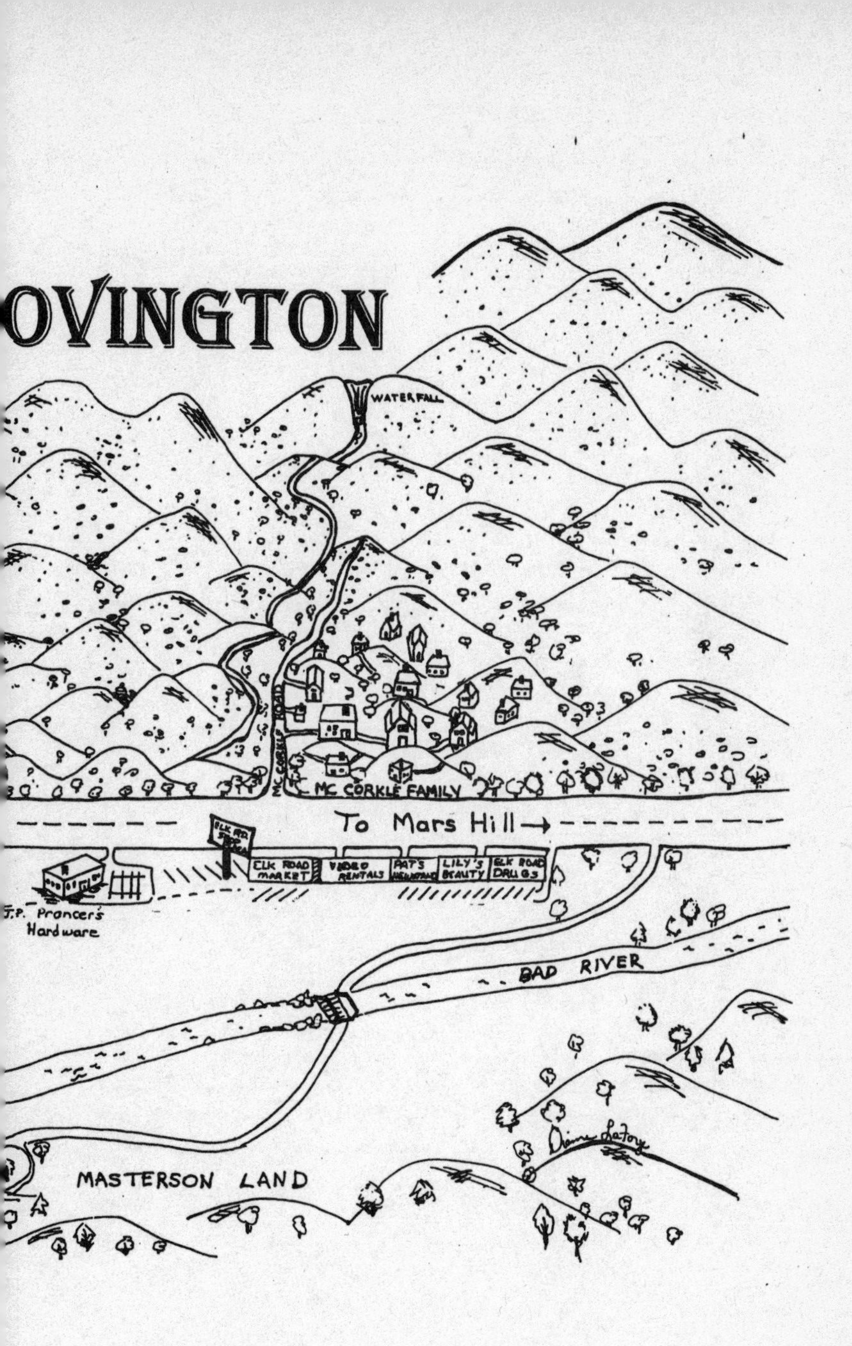

OVINGTON
WATERFALL
MC CORKLE ROAD
MC CORKLE FAMILY
To Mars Hill →
ELK ROAD MARKET
VIDEO RENTALS
PAT'S
LILY'S BEAUTY
ELK ROAD DRUGS
J.P. Prancer's Hardware
BAD RIVER
MASTERSON LAND

One

Unwelcome Visitors

It began as a light snowfall, barely covering the black macadam of Cove Road in Covington. By four o'clock, visibility from the farmhouse windows was restricted to the front bumper of Amelia Declose's car in the driveway. As the world beyond the house darkened, so did the interior of the house.

Amelia switched on the lights and glanced at the kitchen clock: five past four, ten past four, fifteen past four. What if her housemates, Grace Singleton and Hannah Parrish-Maxwell, could not get home? What if the weather closed the roads or they had been in a serious traffic accident? Next door, the fast-falling snow obscured the cottage of Bob Richardson, Grace's significant other, while across the road, George Maxwell's farmhouse was blurred behind a screen of white.

Just glancing outside chilled her, and Amelia jerked the curtains across the kitchen window. Moving through the downstairs rooms, she lowered all the blinds and set the thermostat higher. Then she turned on the light in the living room and flipped the switch in the gas fireplace. Flames sprang to life behind the artificial logs, creating a sense of warmth and welcome.

The ringing of the doorbell, followed by someone knocking at the front door, startled her. *Hannah? Grace? No, they wouldn't ring or knock nor would Max or Bob. They all have keys.*

Amelia peered through the peephole. Standing beside the door, rubbing her bare hands together and blowing into them, stood a young woman with light brown hair. Pressing close and tugging the woman's jacket, a pretty, blond-haired little girl appeared close to tears. The child wore neither hat nor gloves.

The doorbell rang again, shattering the silence in the house.

"Who is it?" Amelia called.

"My name is Miriam Declose-Smith and this is my daughter, Sadie. Is this the home of Amelia Declose?"

With the storm raging outside, Amelia was uncertain that she had heard correctly. "Who did you say you were?" Amelia pressed her ear to the doorjamb. "What did you say? Who did you say you were?"

"My name is Miriam, and I'm Thomas Declose's daughter."

Amelia gasped and lurched back. *Thomas's daughter? Impossible. Our daughter died when she was nine years old.*

The woman's voice was louder now and pleading. "Please, won't you let us in? It's terribly cold out here. I can explain everything."

Surely I heard her wrong. She must be Thomas's cousin, some-

one he rarely saw, forgot to mention? Should I let them come inside? This could be a scam of some kind, and she could be using the child to gain my sympathy.

Amelia squinted through the peephole again. Through the blur of snowflakes, she saw Hannah's husband, Max, stomp up the steps and stand beside the woman. She turned toward him, and they talked for a moment. Then he stamped snow from his boots and brushed the snow from his jacket and red scarf. The flaps of his red cap covered his ears almost to his chin. Max pulled off a leather glove, inserted his key in the lock, and entered the house, shepherding the woman and child before him.

Amelia retreated as if before an invading army. How dare Max escort this lying stranger into her house?

The little girl, no more than seven, walked unselfconsciously toward Amelia. Wide-eyed, she looked up at her. "You're a very pretty lady," she said softly. "Just like in my mama's picture." Her eyes were blue, the same blue as Thomas's and Caroline's. The child extended a small hand, red and chapped from the cold, and smiled. "I'm Sadie Declose-Smith."

Unwittingly, Amelia kneeled beside her, took her hands, and rubbed them gently between her own warm hands. "There, Sadie. That's better, isn't it?"

Sadie smiled. "Yes, thank you. Being in here is much, much warmer. It was so cold outside."

Amelia rose to her feet, her gaze traveling first to the woman's face and then to Max's. *What kind of mother takes a child out in weather like this without a hat and gloves?*

"This young lady claims to be a relative of your husband, Thomas." Max nodded toward Miriam.

"I am his daughter."

Amelia noticed that Miriam's chin quivered. "That's a barefaced lie, if I ever heard one. Who are you? Why did you come here? What do you want?"

Sadie backed away from Amelia, looking frightened. She grasped her mother's hand and snuggled against her, and Amelia regretted having spoken so harshly.

Max turned to Amelia, then glanced at Sadie—implying "watch your language, your tone of voice." "Could we settle this over a cup of tea or coffee? I'm chilled to the bone, and I'm sure these folks are too. Hannah and Grace are stuck over in Weaverville, so they're going to check in at a bed-and-breakfast tonight. A couple of the roads out this way are impassable with high snowdrifts. Bob's staying overnight at Martin's condo. Your phone's out. I know you hate being alone, especially in weather like this, and I thought you might want to stay at my place."

"They should have stayed home! They *knew* we were expecting bad weather." Amelia turned to face the woman. "How did you get here, if the roads are so bad?"

"It wasn't snowing heavily when I arrived. I've been parked down the road for a long while, working up the courage to approach your house."

Max took Amelia's arm and gently urged her toward the kitchen. "I need coffee," he said, and helped himself from the freshly brewed pot on the stove. He poured a cup for the woman, who accepted it and thanked him. Rankled by the way he had come in and taken over, Amelia declined the coffee. This was *her* home, not Max's.

He said, "I didn't believe them when they predicted light snow. This is the kind of storm we expect in March. You can barely see your hand in front of your face out there." Max looked down at Sadie. "Want some milk and cookies, honey?" He lifted Grace's cookie jar from atop the refrigerator and placed it on the kitchen table. "These are some really good homemade cookies."

The little girl looked at her mother.

"You may have a cookie, Sadie," Miriam said.

Sadie reached into the jar and removed one sugar cookie. Her politeness impressed Amelia, who was used to Melissa, Bob's five-year-old granddaughter. She would grab a handful and scamper about the house, dropping crumbs and making a mess that someone else—usually Grace, or the child's father, Russell, if he were here—had to clean up. It was easier than trying to force Melissa to pick up her mess. The child was particularly adept at having temper tantrums.

Max motioned to the woman and child. "Please have a seat. Now, tell us who you are and why you're in Covington." He rounded the kitchen table to where Amelia stood, pulled out a chair and motioned her to sit, which she reluctantly did. "What's this all about?"

The woman addressed Amelia. "I am truly sorry to come here like this. I know this is very difficult to hear and must seem impossible, but my name really is Miriam Declose-Smith. My mother changed her name to Stella Harding-Declose, and my father was Thomas Declose."

Amelia's mouth fell open. She was certain that for a moment her heart stopped.

"Forgive me for intruding on you, for coming here, but I'm desperately in need of your help." Tears filled Miriam's eyes as they traveled from Max to Amelia, then back to Max. "Please, is there somewhere that Sadie can lie down while we talk? I have a storybook in my bag. She could look at the pictures."

Max took the book from Miriam, pulled out the little girl's chair, and reached for her hand. "Come with me, Sadie. We'll go sit on the couch in the living room and I'll read you a story."

Her mother nodded. Sadie hesitated a moment. She looked up at Max, who smiled down at her. Then she took his hand, and they left the room.

The woman's a barefaced liar. I'll confront her, refute her claim, and order her from my home, Amelia thought.

But before she could speak, Miriam said, "It's rather a long story. I'll get to it straightaway."

For the first time, Amelia noted her British accent.

Miriam rummaged in her purse, and extracted a plastic case, which she handed to Amelia.

Amelia stared down at a photo of Thomas, his arm about the shoulders of a pretty young woman with curly brown hair, a woman whom Miriam resembled. The woman's head, tilted to one side, rested on Thomas's shoulder. Trusting eyes looked up at him, and her smile was sweet.

Amelia slammed the photo on the table. "That is my husband, Thomas." Her eyes narrowed; blood pounded at her temples. Soon she would have a splitting headache. "Where did you get it? Who are you? What do you want?"

"I got the picture from my mother, Stella, before she died." Miriam retrieved the photo and slipped it out of Amelia's sight. "I'm sorry, but my father *was* Thomas Declose. He worked for the International Red Cross." In a nervous gesture, she ran her tongue along her lips. "I thought and thought about how best to tell you, but there is no best way, is there? I guess I really botched it. I am so very sorry." She was crying now, tears streaming down her cheeks.

"Wipe your face," Amelia said, her voice hard-edged.

Miriam grabbed a napkin that Max had placed on the table and pressed it against her face. Then she straightened her shoulders and said, "I know what a shock this must be for you, but it's true. Please believe me. I am Stella and Thomas's daughter. I swear I am. I have a birth certificate to prove it. My parents met during the time you lived in Paris when my father traveled regularly to London."

Amelia's body slumped. After Caroline's death Thomas had begun to travel excessively, and was never available when she needed him most. There had been many fights, mainly her screaming at him and him pacing, his hands clasped tightly behind his back, saying nothing, though she had seen the vein in his temple throbbing. After a time, he would leave the house.

Amelia closed her eyes. She could still hear his heavy steps on the landing outside their bedroom, then on the stairs, and finally the slamming of the front door. She would lie in bed alone, feeling miserable and berating herself for having driven him away. Miriam's voice yanked her from her memories.

"Until a few weeks before my mother died, I believed that

my father was a captain in the Queen's navy, and that he had died at sea. I was devastated when my mother confessed to me on her deathbed that my father was a development director for the Red Cross, whom she had met when he was on a trip to London, and that they had been . . . well, involved with one another for over two years." Tears clouded her eyes as she continued.

"I sat there in shock, while my mother explained that her pregnancy had not been planned, and that when she told him that she was pregnant, he made it clear to her that he would never leave you, his wife. She said that he first urged her to have an abortion. They argued about that for a long while."

"An abortion?" The idea appalled Amelia. Still, she took comfort in visualizing Thomas standing over this woman, Stella, who sat weeping in a chain, and saying, "I love my wife, Amelia. You must have an abortion."

"My mother, of course, refused," Miriam said. "He agreed to provide some support. All my growing-up years, we received a check at holiday time—that's all, one check. My mother had said that it came from the navy for my father's war service, a yearly stipend they sent to widows.

"But now, here she was telling me that the money came from my father—your husband. He had extracted a pledge of silence from her in exchange for this, and set up a trust for my college education."

The bitterness in Miriam's voice melted. "I'm not being fair to her. My mother loved him very much. She said he was the great love of her life. She was also a woman of honor and integrity, and she understood what exposure would mean for him, for his career, and what it would do to you. She promised never to write or to phone him or contact him. She was faithful to that promise, and so was I—until now."

Something inside of Amelia crumbled.

Thomas betrayed me? Thomas was unfaithful to me for over two years, and he produced a child? A roar, akin to an ocean pounding on cliffs, filled Amelia's ears, and she covered them with her hands. *This cannot be true. It's a huge lie, concocted by this woman for some bizarre reason.* "You're a liar and a fraud." Amelia's voice sounded strained and hoarse.

Miriam did not move. They faced one another across the table. Neither spoke for a long while, then Miriam said, "I'm not a liar. It is not my fault that I was born. Sadie and I are innocent participants in this . . . this family tragedy."

"We are not family," Amelia said.

Miriam sighed. "I was twenty-two before I knew anything about any of this. After graduating from college in London, I married an American engineer and we lived in Connecticut. Sadie was five years old and I had been teaching part-time when my mother became ill and faced exploratory surgery. I flew home to England at once. We had so little time, she and I. It was just a few weeks before she died.

"When she told me, I was shocked and speechless, I was angry at him and at her, but I loved her, and she was dying. After the shock and the denial and anger wore off, I wanted to dash out and find my father, but my mother extracted a promise that I would honor her pledge to him. It was not easy for me to come here, and I am sorry I had to. I had no place to turn. I kept reminding myself that my mother thought so highly of you, Mrs. Declose. She said you were a very special woman, someone so good and loving that my father would never leave you, not even for her and me.

"She gave me the address she had for him in Paris, and she made me promise to use it only in the most dire of circumstances. When I finally used it, the address was very old, but I knew he was with the Red Cross. When I grew desperate in my situation with Darren, I hired someone to find my father and ended up with an address in New Jersey, a place called Silver Lake. Then, things improved at home, the beatings stopped . . ."

Amelia gasped. *Beatings? Who beat her? Did someone strike that little girl?*

"Darren, my ex-husband, changed jobs. For a while he was happier, so life was less traumatic for a time . . ." Her voice trailed off and she was silent for a few moments. "I shoved the address into my jewelry box, thinking that perhaps I would never need it. Many times, over the last few years, I held that paper in my hand, but each time something stopped me from using it, and I would tuck it back into the box."

Miriam placed two more photos on the table, where they lay like barriers between them. "This is the only picture I have of my parents together. This other photo, the one of my father and you, is the one that Sadie referred to when she first saw you. My mother said that she had sneaked it from his wallet."

Amelia studied Miriam for any resemblance to Thomas,

but saw none in the young woman's light brown eyes and hair, her high forehead and cheekbones, or the shape of her mouth. It was Sadie, with her blue eyes and fair hair, her tiny cleft chin, who resembled Thomas.

If this story is true, what does she want from me? Money?

Miriam had spoken simply, seemingly from the heart, but scam artists could do that. Still, it had the ring of truth, and Amelia's heart raced. She stared at the photo, unmistakably of Thomas and an attractive woman who strongly resembled Miriam.

Was it possible that the husband she had devoted her life to, whom she had trusted, had been involved with this woman? Was it possible that he had *loved* her? That idea was incredibly painful, and Amelia stifled the urge to snatch up the photo and tear it into bits.

That won't change anything. It is definitely Thomas. I haven't seen a picture of him in years, not since the fire destroyed our home and I lost almost everything. He was so handsome. He looks so young, smiling and happy. And he's with another woman. She winced and closed her eyes. *Is it possible this young woman is telling the truth?*

Amelia's hands pressed against her stomach. It was hard to breathe, to keep from kicking the table, throwing a chair, screaming, ordering the woman from her house.

Caroline! Her daughter's name flashed like a neon sign across her mind. Amelia took a deep breath. After Caroline died, Amelia had failed to conceive again, not for lack of trying. The disappointment month after month was stressful. Several times, they had discussed adoption. Thomas's work with the Red Cross brought them in contact with so many orphans, but he had adamantly resisted that idea and Amelia had resigned herself to being childless.

In her muddled state, Amelia struggled but failed to put dates to those years when they had tried so hard, when month after month she had wept into his shoulder. Was that when he had taken a mistress and fathered a child? How could he have *done* this to her? She had been duped, used, lied to! The very idea that if he were alive today, Thomas would have a child of his own and a beautiful granddaughter, and she had no family, none at all, was mind numbing and unbearable. She hated him, *hated* Thomas for his betrayal of her, hated herself for her gullibility. But most of all, she hated this woman and her child, who had appeared out of nowhere to torture her.

Amelia pressed her hands against her pressured temples. Then, struggling to stifle sobs, she lowered her head onto the table.

Go away, you awful woman! When I lift my head you'll be gone, and this last hour will all have been a bad dream.

Max's laughter, followed by the light laugh of the child, drifted in from the living room. This was no dream.

"What do you want?" Amelia asked, not lifting her head.

Miriam leaned across the table, and Amelia smelled the faintest trace of lavender. "A place to hide," she whispered.

Amelia raised her head and stared in disbelief at the young woman. For a moment, her spirits lifted. Miriam was a criminal fleeing from the law, or maybe a psychiatric patient escaped from a hospital. "Hide from whom? Who are you running away from? What have you done?"

Miriam's shoulders sagged; she seemed on the verge of collapsing. "I haven't done anything but run for my life and Sadie's life." Her hands, resting on the table, curled into fists. "My husband, Darren Smith, was physically abusive and growing more violent all the time. I was terrified that he would hurt Sadie, too, so I ran away to a shelter. They were kind to me. They helped me, and after a truly frightening time, with counseling and good legal assistance, I was able to get a divorce."

Her voice tightened, but she took a sip of coffee, gained a measure of control, and continued. "I thought I was free of him. We had a restraining order, but Darren ignored it. A month ago, he broke into the house where we were living and he beat me. Sadie saw it. It was the first, the only time she'd seen me being thrown against a wall, slapped, and kicked. She stood there screaming. That was the worst of it for me—worse than his fists."

Miriam's voice cracked. "He threatened Sadie, said that if she said anything to anyone, he'd come back and kill us both. We left that night, drove to another state, holed up in a motel, and started looking for my fa . . . for Thomas Declose. When I discovered he had died, I didn't know where to turn, or what to do. I have no one—no aunts or uncles, no one. Only you, if you will help us, just for a little while . . ." Her voice trailed off. "I am so tired and so frightened."

An empty silence followed.

"How did you find me?" Amelia asked. She would not let this woman wheedle sympathy from her.

"The search agency that I hired to locate my father sent

me your address in Pennsylvania, and I persuaded the woman who answered the phone to at least tell me that you had moved to Covington, North Carolina. Your name and address are in the phone book. We drove down and stayed for a week at the motel in Mars Hill. We drove past your home many times, but I hadn't the nerve to ring your doorbell." Miriam paused and wiped her eyes with the napkin. "I am so sorry I've caused you pain. I took a huge chance in coming here, but I'm desperate. I hoped that since my mother and your husband are both dead, you might understand and help me."

Understand? You expect me to understand? "Help you how?"

"By letting us stay with you for a week or two, until I can figure out what to do, where to go. I have a little money, but I need to find work and a place to live where Sadie will be safe."

Under different circumstances, Amelia would have opened her home and heart to Miriam, but Thomas's breach of faith outweighed that. "You can't stay here," she said.

"She can stay at my place." Max's large frame filled the doorway to the kitchen.

Amelia stared at him. No, she wanted to yell. No.

Max looked at Miriam. "Sadie's asleep on the couch. I heard some of your story. If there's one thing I detest, it's a man who beats up on a woman. You and Sadie can come home with me, stay as long as you'd like. We have plenty of room—three extra bedrooms."

Miriam had risen and stood with one hand on the back of the chair as if for support.

"I'm like family," he assured her. "I'm married to Amelia's friend Hannah, and I live just across the street. My housekeeper, Anna, will have a big pot of stew ready for everyone. Amelia, how about a blanket to cover Sadie? I'll carry her."

At Amelia's nod, Miriam hesitantly said, "Thank you. What about my car?" She glanced at Amelia.

"Leave it in the driveway here," Max said. "We'll sort it all out after the storm. What about you, Amelia? Are you coming? This is gonna go on all night. I don't want to leave you here alone."

Amelia shook her head. "I'm not going anywhere." She walked out of the kitchen and returned with a blanket, which she handed to Miriam, who wrapped it about her daughter.

Even in sleep Sadie looks like Thomas. "Cover her head, Max, and wrap her up tight," Amelia heard herself say.

Max pointed to the umbrella stand by the front door. "Take one, Miriam. It'll at least keep the snow off your head." He turned back to Amelia. "It's gonna be dark and very cold if the electric goes out, and it's bound to. I have a generator. You ought to come with us. I don't want to leave you here like this."

She shook her head. "I'd rather not. I'll be fine. You go."

"I'll leave my front door unlocked in case you change your mind. If you come over, be sure you wear high boots. Bundle up good and use a strong flashlight. It's slippery out there, and dark."

Amelia didn't care if she froze, or if she died that very moment. She wanted them *gone.*

They stepped from the porch and vanished into the white

snow that separated her from the rest of the world, her friendly world now suddenly turned unbearably painful.

Amelia locked the front door, the back door, and all the windows. At the foot of the stairs, she grasped the railing for support. She felt old, incredibly tired, and as drained and disoriented as she had been in those terrible days following Thomas's death.

She couldn't climb the stairs tonight. Turning, she walked slowly into the living room and sank down onto the couch.

Two

The Past Is Past, or Is It?

Amelia lay on the couch, not caring if her shoes smudged the light-colored fabric, or if the down pillows tumbled onto the floor. Outside the house, the storm raged; within the house, Amelia raged—one moment assuring herself that the woman was a fraud and a liar, and the next moment knowing in her gut that Miriam's story was true.

Amelia pressed a pillow against her chest and rocked back and forth, back and forth, weeping. After a long while, her sobs slowed, then ceased. Rising slowly off the couch, she went to the kitchen for a glass of water, drank deeply, and splashed her face with cool water. Violent gusts of wind hurled snow against the windowpane, blurring visibility.

The lights from Max's house, so familiar and reassuring, were no longer discernible, and Amelia wondered what he and his houseguests were doing. Were they sitting around the table in the big, warm kitchen eating Anna's wonderful stew? Which of the unused bedrooms had Max assigned to them? Loneliness swept over her and she stepped back from the window. Why speculate? What did she care, anyway?

Returning to the living room, she sank again onto the couch. Memories of Thomas and their life together sped through her mind. She found it hard to focus, to grab hold of specific events in their lives. What might he have done or said that should have aroused her suspicion? Nothing came to mind. Nothing pushed its way through the blur of thoughts! He had been so adroit at diplomacy—that was his job, after all—and so attentive and solicitous of her. Ignorant of his double life, Amelia had filled her days with activities and friends. They had been a team. She had devoted herself to planning the most glamorous dinners for people whom he hoped would later make generous contributions to the Red Cross. Never for a moment had she considered that Thomas was anything but a faithful and loving husband.

There was some small comfort in the fact that for many years, she had been spared the appalling truth of Thomas' infidelity. On the other hand, during those years she had been lied to, deceived, and betrayed, and that galled her now.

If he had told her, how would she have reacted, and what would have been the outcome?

Maybe he would have told her over a dinner of roast beef and Yorkshire pudding, his favorite meal. She pictured Thomas setting down his wineglass, his expression doleful. Speaking slowly, he would pour out his devastating tale: how he had met a woman, how he never intended it to happen, and on and on. In one scenario he declared his love for Amelia, in another he declared his passion for Miriam's mother. The thought of his loving another woman hurt so badly that she clutched a pillow and bent over it, pressing it to her middle.

Yet another vignette found them in bed. They had often sat shoulder to shoulder in their king-sized bed at night, she reading a novel, he engrossed in material from the office. Thomas reached over, took her hand in his and slowly, sadly related the story that tore her heart to shreds. Her reactions followed: screaming and yelling, beating her fists against his chest. Or would she be doubled over, struck dumb by his confession?

Would she have stayed with him? Could she ever have forgiven him? She thought not. Perhaps she would have been cunning and stayed with him, the unforgiving wife, squeezing from him every last ounce of guilt. Or perhaps she would have divorced Thomas and created a scandal, designed to end his career with the International Red Cross. Surely she would have terminated the role she played as the compliant helpmate and gracious hostess.

Amelia shivered and wrapped her arms about her shoulders. There was another possibility. What if, when he confessed his affair, she had none of those choices? What if he confessed and then had announced that he was leaving her?

She sighed deeply. Ignorance had indeed been bliss.

Why had Thomas done such a thing? Had losing their daughter precipitated his infidelity? She remembered him as a wonderful and devoted husband, and she spoke to Grace and Hannah as if her life with him had been near perfect. The truth was, she had often regretted her too-early marriage, and more than once she had struggled with the decision whether to leave Thomas. With all his traveling, the ever-changing homes, and his being a workaholic, her life had often been unsatisfying, unhappy, and lonely.

After Caroline died, during those days and nights while he buried himself in work to forget his pain, she had considered leaving him, but she'd felt there was no place to go. With no college education, she'd deemed herself unemployable.

The lights flickered, then failed, plunging the house into darkness, the fireplace now her sole source of light and heat. The wind snarled at the eaves and rattled the windows with what seemed like rage.

Trees that bend before an onslaught don't break.

Amelia imagined herself as a tree bending in the face of a high wind. Had she not survived the death of her only child? Had she not survived the car crash that killed Thomas and left her with burns on her neck and shoulder? Had she not survived loneliness and depression so terrible that she had turned to a psychiatrist for help?

Yes, indeed, she had bent before many a storm. She would bend before this one, and she would survive.

She whispered a prayer of thanks for Grace and Hannah, whom she had met at Olive Pruitt's dreary boardinghouse in Pennsylvania. That meeting changed her life. Their friendship had given her hope; their trust and encouragement had bolstered her courage. She had become a new, vibrant, creative person after knowing them.

Her eyes traveled to the living room ceiling as if expecting to see Thomas peering down at her from above. "I'm happy. I'm happy, do you hear me?" she yelled. "I share a home with Grace and Hannah, the sisters I never had. I'm a successful photographer. My work is shown in a New York gallery. People buy my photographs, and I've published two coffee-table books. Look at me, Thomas, wherever you are! I'm not the dependent, insecure woman that you knew. I've made it without you. I'm a person in my own right, and I *don't* have to forgive you or take in your illegitimate daughter and her child."

Amelia pushed up from the couch, made her way to the guest room and returned with the down comforter. As she pulled it over her on the couch and waited for it to wrap her in its warmth, it struck her that the past was just that: the past. Yes, she was deeply hurt and humiliated to think that Thomas had wanted another woman, had slept with another woman, had conceived a child with another woman.

But time healed: she knew that from bitter experience. She would need time to sort it all out, to move beyond the shock and searing hurt, but she was resilient. And somehow, with help from her friends, she would get past this. Peace gradually came over Amelia, and she fell asleep.

Someone was shaking her. Amelia opened her eyes. The blinds had been raised and bright light filtered through the lace curtains. Her shoulders and neck ached from her cramped position on the couch.

Grace bent over her, a worried expression on her face. "Amelia. Wake up. Look, the sun's out. It's warming up fast, and the snow's starting to melt, thank goodness. I dropped

Hannah off at Max's a few minutes ago. He told us briefly about what happened, about Miriam and the child. My Lord, Amelia, what a terrible shock that must have been for you. I'm so sorry you were alone. How are you?"

Amelia massaged her neck, then ran her fingers though her hair. "I'm not too bad, considering. It hurt so much—a terrible blow to the gut." She rested her hands on her stomach. "I don't know when anything hurt that much." She held out a hand to Grace for support, swung her legs off the couch, and bent to rub them.

"I'm too old to sleep on a couch. Too old for all this stress and aggravation. Last night was just awful, and strange, too. I went from being devastated and enraged enough to explode, to feeling almost indifferent. That's odd, isn't it?" She leaned back against the couch cushions. "Did you see the child? She's the spitting image of Thomas, even to that cleft in her chin. That was the worst of it, Grace—she looks so much like Caroline and Thomas."

Tears filled her eyes, and she blinked them away. "I'm not saying that I'm over it. It's horrendous, suddenly having to face the truth that half of my married life was a lie. In time, I'm sure I'll adjust to the idea." Then suddenly she wasn't so sure. "Do you think I will, Grace?"

"Of course you will. And as you say, it happened a long time ago, and you were spared knowing about it all these years."

"I just don't want them around me," Amelia said. "Let them stay at Max's. I don't care if I never lay eyes on them again." *Though why am I drawn to that little girl—because she looks like my Caroline? Or is my memory playing tricks on me?*

Several years ago, when the farmhouse burned, Amelia had lost all but one small faded snapshot of her daughter, which had been in her wallet. Of all the losses from that fire—many of her irreplaceable antique fans, her clothing, furniture, everything—it was the album of her daughter's pictures that she had most grieved for and still did, these many years later.

"Did you see the child?" she asked.

"No, I didn't," Grace said. "I was in a hurry to get home to you. Come on. Go freshen up and change your clothes. Let me make you some breakfast."

"You're so good to me, Grace. What would I do without you?" Amelia unsteadily stood and embraced Grace, holding her close. "You're my family, and I love you."

"I love you, too. Now go on, wash up and change." Grace pointed toward the stairs.

Amelia did not return to the kitchen for breakfast. Torn between the desire to respect her privacy and the hope that this was not the beginning of a severe depression, like the one Amelia had experienced after the fire destroyed their home, Grace finally ate breakfast alone.

The hours passed. Grace folded a stack of towels that had been left piled atop the table near the dryer in the laundry room. She swept and mopped the kitchen floor. She started a pot of chicken soup, just the thing for a chilly day like this. Once she tiptoed upstairs and placed her ear against Amelia's bedroom door, but heard nothing. Figuring Amelia was asleep, Grace retreated downstairs. Taking a cup of tea, she went into the guest room and turned on the television to her favorite House and Garden channel, and still the hours seemed endless.

Later, Grace heard the front door open and recognized Hannah's footsteps in the foyer. She immediately shut off the television and went to join her friend in the kitchen.

Hannah had placed a pot of water for tea on the stove. "How's Amelia?" she asked.

"It's hard to tell," Grace replied. "When I came home, she was asleep on the living room couch. When she woke up, she claimed to be just fine. But how could she be, really?"

"Thomas is past history. His affair with Miriam's mother is past history. The quicker Amelia accepts that fact and lets it go, the better off she'll be. Where is she?"

"Upstairs." Grace considered Hannah's appraisal of the situation a trifle harsh, even if she agreed with her premise.

"It couldn't have been comfortable sleeping on that couch in the cold," Hannah said. "Max wanted her to go over there with them, but would she go? No. It must have been freezing over here last night. That single fireplace couldn't possibly have kept her comfortable. Thank God the lights came on so fast."

"She was covered with a comforter," Grace said. "What would you have had her do, Hannah? Amelia was devastated. I can understand her not wanting to be with Miriam, and needing to be alone. Can't you?"

Hannah shrugged. "I guess so. But to stay here alone, knowing that the electricity was bound to go out as it always does in a winter storm, is rather foolish." Hannah accepted the cup of tea, to which Grace had added cream and sugar.

"Tell me, Hannah, do you like them, the woman and her child?"

"Yes, I do. Miriam seems like a decent sort of person, and the little girl is very well mannered."

"We have to do something about Amelia," Grace said. "She's . . ."

"What do you propose that we do?" Hannah pulled out a chair at the table and sank into it.

"I'm not sure, but I can't stand by and let her sink into another depression. I've canceled my dinner with Bob tonight. I don't want to leave her alone. She's been in her room all day. I want to be here when she gets up, in case she needs me."

Hannah rolled her eyes. "She's been in her room all day? Isn't that a bit melodramatic? This isn't quite the same as losing everything she owned in a fire."

Grace stared at her in surprise. "No, I don't think Amelia's being melodramatic. She's done a lot of thinking and seemed quite reasonable when I spoke to her. And of course it's not the same as after the fire, but surely you can see how crushing and, well, humiliating this is for her."

Hannah threw up her hands. "You're much kinder than I am, Grace. The way I look at it, Amelia could wallow in this way beyond what's necessary. She's been known to do that. That's all I'm saying."

"I find that incredibly callous, Hannah. If it were me, I'd be just as furious and upset as Amelia is. I'd want to kill Ted, even if he is dead, if I found out that he had had an affair and a child with another woman."

Hannah set down her teacup. "You're right, of course. You usually are. I'm sorry I sounded so hard-hearted. It's just that Thomas's affair with Miriam's mother happened over twenty-five years ago, and Miriam didn't have anything to do with it. They're here now, and they need her help, our help. Max has offered them his home for as long as they need it, and that's fine with me." Hannah pushed back her chair. "I'm going up to shower and change, and then I'm going back over to Max's. I'll be there for dinner if you need me."

Grace followed Hannah to the foot of the stairs. "Do you believe Miriam's story? What if it's not true?"

Hannah's foot rested on the bottom step; she turned to face Grace. "I believe what she's saying. Max does also. If she's lying, she's well rehearsed and a darn good actress, and she's got those pictures."

"Couldn't she have obtained them somehow? Couldn't this be a plot to get money from Amelia?" Grace asked. "I almost wish it were. That way, Amelia wouldn't feel so shattered and humiliated."

"To be cautious, Max is having a police check and a credit check run on Miriam, and on that husband she claims she ran away from," Hannah said. "He's checking on her mother, also. She gave him the dates of her birth and death and where she's buried."

"All anyone has to do is go to the graveyard and get that information off a tombstone," Grace said.

"You've been watching way too many mysteries on the

BBC station, Grace. Given time, Amelia will be just fine. Maybe she'll even get to like Miriam and Sadie." Hannah climbed the stairs and disappeared into her bedroom at the front of the house, across the hall from Amelia's room. Grace, feeling worried, returned to the kitchen.

When Hannah came back downstairs and poked her head into the kitchen, Grace was intent on rolling out dough she had prepared earlier. A variety of cookie cutters, stars, trees, and animals, lay close at hand.

"Hey, Grace, smile. It's going to be fine. I'd stay, but Amelia would much rather have you than me around. If you need me or Max, all you have to do is call and we'll be here in a jiffy."

Three

Grace to the Rescue

Feeling listless and melancholy, Amelia had spent her day in a darkened bedroom. Periodically she dozed and awakened with a heavy heart. At one point hunger assailed her, but that had passed. She intended to shower and change her clothing and to join Grace downstairs, but lethargy had weighted her like ballast.

Once she thought she heard Hannah's footsteps and she waited, thinking that Hannah might knock or come into the room, but she had not, which had further saddened Amelia. Maybe it was best that way. Hannah needn't say a word for Amelia to sense her impatience and disapproval. Hannah coped by stifling emotions and burying herself in work. That's what she had done after the fire. "Up and out and on with it" could be Hannah's motto.

Amelia was not prepared to forget Thomas's behavior or to forgive him, nor was she prepared to stuff down her resentment and the anger she felt toward Miriam. She was not going to plaster a smile on her face and act as if everything was hunky-dory. It was not!

With Hannah gone, Grace could no longer tolerate the lonely silence. She prepared a tray of cucumber and cream cheese finger sandwiches and a pot of tea and carried it upstairs. Holding the tray on one hip, Grace knocked on Amelia's door, and entered.

Amelia mumbled, "Thank you, Grace. Just leave it on my dresser. I'll get up soon."

Grace placed the tray on the dresser. "I'm not going to leave you alone. I'm going to open the curtains and let the light in. It's late afternoon and it's warmed up considerably. Get up, and we'll have our tea and sandwiches on the porch. There's the making of a gorgeous sunset out there." She went to the window. "Look. The sky's turning a most beautiful pumpkin color."

"Not today." Amelia rolled over and buried her head in her pillow. "I'll sit outside with you tomorrow."

"No, Amelia, today. Now!"

Amelia lifted her head. "What did you say?"

Grace sat on the side of the bed beside Amelia. "You're devastated, and I understand that. But no one close to you has died, even though it may feel as if Thomas has all over again. But he hasn't. We're not even sure that Miriam is telling the truth. Max is having her checked out, and her mother, too."

"I've thought about it a lot, and I doubt she's lying," Amelia said. "The little girl looks too much like Thomas."

"Either way it's been a terrible shock to your system, and

it's even harder to cope with a blow like this as we grow older. But not eating and giving in to self-pity will lower your resistance, and you'll get sick."

Slowly, Amelia swung her legs over the side of the bed and sat up. It frightened Grace how she seemed to have aged so much in only one day. Her shoulders slumped. Her hair lay matted about her face, and dark circles framed her turquoise-blue eyes, which had lost their vibrancy.

Amelia pushed a thick lock of hair off her forehead. "I feel totally depleted of energy, as if I'll never be able to pick up my camera and photograph again." She raised her arms and let them drop to her side. "They feel like chunks of wood. I feel like a chunk of wood."

"It's normal to react like this to the shock you've had. I'd feel the same exact way if someone walked in here and announced that she was Ted's daughter."

"You would?"

"Of course I would! I'd be furious and disappointed, and I'd feel betrayed, and rightly so. Any woman would."

"Last night I was able to say the past is the past. But today . . ." Amelia's eyes narrowed. "Today I hate Thomas, and Miriam, and even the child. How could he have done this to me, Grace?" Amelia covered her face with her hands, and began to cry.

Cry it out, Grace thought, *cry it out. Then you'll get up, and we'll go downstairs.*

After a time, Amelia wiped her eyes with the sheet. "You're right, of course. When you consider all the things we've been through, the people we've loved and lost, we can survive whatever life dishes out, can't we? This came at me out of the blue, that's all. And whatever Thomas did, it's not the fault of that woman and child, is it?"

"No. It really isn't."

Amelia's eyes clouded, and she nibbled at her lower lip. "Grace, I just thought of something. What if that dreadful ex-husband of Miriam's hunts for her and finds her here?"

Violence terrified Amelia, perhaps because of a movie that her nanny had taken her to when she was eight years old. They had both covered their eyes and ears and hastened from the theater, but not before an impressionable Amelia saw screaming men shot and stabbed, and blood flowing in the movie street. She had never been able to permanently erase that memory or the fears it had fostered.

Grace waved her hand, dismissing Amelia's concern. "How is he going to find her? We're about as far off the beaten path as anyone can get."

"There are more isolated places—like Old Bunkie Creek, where the Inman family live, or down in South Carolina where Roger lives."

"The Inmans? You mean the people who had that terrible flood, whom you photographed for your book last year?" Grace asked.

Amelia nodded.

"You're right. That really *is* off the beaten path." Grace picked up the tray. "Let's go down and see that sunset."

They started for the door, but Amelia stopped. "If *we* lived way back on Old Bunkie Creek, accessible only by a rutted, dirt road, no one could find us."

"What a dreadful thought." Inwardly, Grace smiled. *The heck she hates that woman and child.*

Four

Healing Oneself in a Disordered World

They wrapped chenille throws about their shoulders and settled the wicker rocking chairs on the front porch. The sunset had marshaled shades of rose, cerise, peach, and pumpkin and woven them into a spectacular kaleidoscope of color. As they watched, awestruck, a sense of peace settled over Amelia.

"I'm so happy you made me get out of bed and come down here, Grace. What a loss it would have been if I had missed a moment of this sunset. I don't think I've ever seen anything quite like it, have you?" She turned to Grace and reaching out with her hand slowed Grace's rocker. Her voice was quiet, almost a whisper, and filled with longing. "I don't want it to end, Grace. I want us to sit here, just like this, feeling like this, forever."

They were still a moment, then Grace said, "Wouldn't it

be wonderful if we had a movie of all the special moments we wished would last forever? It would perk us up when our spirits were low, make us happy when we felt unhappy, remind us that our lives have been touched by great beauty, love, and joy. It's so easy to forget those things, to get caught up in life's aggravations."

"What a great idea. And we could have music to go along with the visuals. I'd choose overtures and music from various operas. Exciting dramatic music, like Wagner's 'The Ride of the Valkyries.' What kind of music would you choose, Grace?"

"Jazz maybe, or Rosemary Clooney singing softly. I don't know. I'd have to experiment."

Amelia reached for another sandwich. "Have some of these, Grace. They're so good, I'm eating them all."

"I made them for you. You haven't eaten all day. I cooked a pot of chicken soup earlier, and had some for lunch and for an early supper, but there's plenty left. Finish the sandwiches. If you want some of the soup later, I'll heat it up for you."

"Will you mash the carrots and cut the chicken into small pieces for me?" Amelia laughed lightly. Grace had trained them to add rice or noodles, chicken, and mashed cooked carrots to their soup, making it a complete meal. She'd never eaten chicken soup that way before. Her mother had served soup only as a clear broth. It had seemed strange at first, all those things in the soup, but Amelia now loved it.

"Thanks for the sandwiches. Your friendship has nurtured me today. I'm so thankful for you and Hannah. Where is she, anyway? Is she coming home for dinner? I thought I heard her earlier."

"Hannah came home for a short while, then dashed back out. She said to call her if you need her and she'd be right over."

"That was nice of her. I know her life gets all caught up with Max, and now he's got Miriam and Sadie staying over there. I guess he wants Hannah to help him with that situation."

"I was thinking," Grace said. "You know when someone asks when you last had a good belly laugh, and you go blank? Why don't I remember when that was? If we could see ourselves giggling, or bent over laughing, in a home movie, we'd remember it and maybe even laugh again."

"You're absolutely right. Someone *did* ask me recently when I'd last had a good laugh, and for the life of me, I couldn't remember. Why would we forget something as pleasant as that?"

"I wish I knew."

All about them, the fading light cast a scrim of gold over the fields, hills, trees, and the houses on Cove Road. "I ought to be taking photographs. This light's perfect. But I don't want to move," Amelia said.

"Don't, then. For a change, be a passive observer."

"I like that." Amelia laughed. "See, I just laughed, and I feel lighthearted instead of heavyhearted." She rocked for a few moments, then stopped. "A passive observer. Isn't that what I was, all those years I was married to Thomas? I entertained for him, involved myself in activities for the Red Cross because he said I ought to. Where was *I*, Amelia, in all of that?"

Grace studied Amelia. Was she about to crash back into depression? "I didn't go to college, and I may not be as smart as some folks. But my experiences and things I've read have led me to believe that everything that happens to us contributes to who we are. Each event, with all its emotions, its ups and downs, builds on another, and prepares us for today. You are wiser, stronger, more self-confident, and more secure than you were when I first met you. You can, and you will, handle this."

"Things go along smoothly for a time, it seems," Amelia said. "You're driving along peacefully and suddenly there's a rockslide. Boulders crash down all about you, some strike you, and you know you must get past them. Things never stay the same, much as we want them to, and I hate that. Don't you?"

Grace nodded. "I guess everyone does. When we're happy, we grow complacent and expect stability and stasis; we want everything to stay as it is. Unfortunately, things rarely stay the same. I don't know why."

Amelia gazed out at the fading sunset.

"To a great extent, life seems to be about coping with one problem after the other, either about people or things," Grace said. "The blessing, I believe, is that as we grow older and hopefully wiser, we become better at figuring out how to cope. I also believe that as we learn from experiences, we develop a broader and more tolerant view of things and people."

"More accepting, you mean?" Amelia asked.

Grace nodded. "Yes. And I think that reacting too quickly

is not always our best course of action. I find, for me, that stepping back and waiting a bit before responding or doing anything works best."

"Are you suggesting that I should not make a hasty decision about Miriam?" Amelia asked.

"What do you think?"

"That you're trying to tell me not to write her off, based on my initial reactions to her."

"Yes, I guess I am. And in the process, you're called upon to do a lot of self-healing."

"Self-healing?"

"I don't know what else to call it. Think about it. When we're little, we depend on our parents to fix things, to heal us. They kiss our wounds, and say soothing words that reassure us that things will be better," Grace said.

"Then we grow up, and there's no parent to reassure us. Hopefully, as mature adults we've found ways to heal ourselves physically and emotionally."

"I've always thought that confession for Catholics must be so comforting," Amelia said.

"It probably is. But not everyone has access to priests and confessionals."

"So we can turn to a good friend, someone we trust," Amelia said. "A friend like you, for instance."

"True. Though I wasn't here last night. And how about people who may not have a good friend? What do they do?"

"In that circumstance, I turned to a psychiatrist for help," Amelia said.

"Thank God for therapists," Grace replied. "But there are

people who won't go to any kind of counselor. What do they do?"

"Well." Amelia leaned forward, her elbow on her knee, her chin on her fist. "Are you saying that sometimes we must to be able to take care of ourselves, to heal ourselves?"

Grace nodded. "Not that I've mastered this art myself. But I'm working on it, and I think you are, too."

"I am?"

"Yes, certainly. What did you do last night? You didn't pace the floor and spend the night stewing. You could have. At another time, you might have. You didn't drink yourself into a stupor, or eat yourself sick. You turned on the fireplace and got warm under that comforter, and you reasoned things out until you felt better. You soothed yourself, Amelia, and then you fell asleep."

Amelia smiled. "I did, didn't I? But I didn't have any option. I couldn't use the phone to call anyone, and I couldn't drive anywhere. I was trapped in the house by myself."

"You could have concentrated on all the negatives until you sent your blood pressure soaring. But you didn't, did you?"

Amelia shook her head.

"You calmed yourself, and that's what I call self-healing."

"I thought I was just being realistic, but I like your self-healing concept. There's strength in that."

"Indeed there is," Grace replied. "Believe me, I'm no expert at this. I read about it somewhere, and it struck me as important and positive to think in those terms."

"But I stayed in bed all day today," Amelia persisted.

"That was healing, too. You've had a terrible shock to your system and you needed the rest. Later, when I asked you to come down with me, you did."

Amelia smiled. "You know, Grace, I never think of myself as a particularly strong person. When I was an adolescent, I overheard my mother telling my aunt that she worried I was so scattered I'd never be able to take care of myself. They both hoped I'd find a man who would look after me. I sometimes think that set the tone for how I saw myself, as fragmented and dependent. Acting cool and sophisticated is just a cover-up, and you know that." She leaned over and gave Grace a hug. "I love you. You are my dearest friend, Grace Singleton."

"And I love you. You're strong, Amelia, and a good, kindhearted woman. In time, you'll sort it all out and do what's right."

"You mean about Miriam and Sadie?"

"Not specifically, but I'm sure you'll handle this business with them as beautifully as you handle everything," Grace said.

"You flatter me. I've messed up so many things."

"And you've *not* messed up many other things, so be positive. Perhaps they'll leave Covington, and you'll never have to see them again. Maybe they'll stay in the area, and you still don't ever have to see them. Or maybe you'll come to care about them and draw them into your circle of friends. Whatever you decide, I'm sure that you will handle it in the best possible manner."

"You're suggesting that I embrace them, even invite them

to move in with us?" Amelia asked, but there was no rancor in her voice.

"Of course not. I'm suggesting that you follow the inclinations of your heart. I also know that you need time, and I'm not suggesting that you rush to any decision. Just let yourself be open and see where it goes."

The inclinations of your heart. That impulse had not always served Amelia well. She didn't think about the accident that had killed Thomas often, but when she did, it was as vivid as if it had happened yesterday and not almost ten years ago. The impact of the car that hit them had wrenched her seat belt from her and pitched her forward into the glare and heat of fire. The wail of an ambulance siren still made her heart thud.

In the hospital, days passed before anyone told her that Thomas had not survived. Her impulse then had been to flee, and once released from the hospital, she had acted on that inclination by selling their New Jersey home, a house that would be worth a fortune today, located a block from the ocean. She had used too much of the money to escape to Europe, where she and Thomas had lived most of their married life.

What came next was blurred: returning to the States, a nervous breakdown, hospitalization. On her release, in greatly reduced financial circumstances, her psychiatrist had suggested Olive Pruitt's Boarding House in Branston, Pennsylvania.

"You need time to rest and recover and not be alone while

you're doing it," he'd said as he handed her Olive's address and phone number.

To this day she blessed him for the information on that slip of paper, for it had led to Hannah and Grace and then to Covington.

Later there was Lance Lundquist, right here in Covington. She had succumbed to his flattery and had conducted herself in a juvenile, ludicrous manner. As Hannah predicted, Lance turned out to be mean, controlling, and self-centered, a man who preyed on gullible, insecure, and foolish women—as she had been.

Grace was suggesting that she honor her inclinations regarding Miriam and her daughter. Instinctively she had been touched by the child, had warmed to her immediately and then withdrawn. As for Miriam, it was hard to tell since she had been the bearer of such shattering information.

Amelia glanced up at the sky and gasped, then rose from her chair to lean against a post. "Look, Grace. It's turning lavender and mauve, with the palest hint of yellow. Have you ever seen anything like it?"

"No, I've never seen a sunset like this one tonight. I'm glad we could share it."

"So am I."

They watched as the sky darkened to a deep midnight blue and a half-moon rose and hung above the hilltop behind Max's house, its edge as smooth and clean as if someone had cut the moon down the middle with a sharp scissors.

The downstairs lights in Max's house went on, and they saw Anna, Max, and Hannah moving about. Then the lights came on in the cottage behind Cove Road Church, where Pastor Johnson had lived for so many years, and where Pastor Dennie Ledbetter now lived. Shortly after, the headlights of Frank Craine's pickup cast wide beams of light as he slowly drove down Cove Road. Frank waved, and Grace and Amelia returned his greeting.

"I feel so at home in Covington," Amelia said. "Remember how standoffish folks were when we first moved here? And then the fire happened, and all the homes on our side of Cove Road were destroyed. It's so sad that it took such a dreadful loss for everyone on the road to become friends. Why must it be like that? We were the same people before the fire as we were afterward."

Grace nodded. Everyone needed that sense of belonging, but Amelia now more than ever. She trusted that in time Amelia would settle the blame for this painful betrayal on Thomas, where it belonged, and not on Miriam and Sadie. Having met neither mother nor daughter, Grace could only go by Hannah's impression, and Hannah, with her cautious and critical approach to things and people, liked them. Amelia was the only one of the three of them who had no family, and Grace, perpetual romantic that she was, wanted Amelia to embrace the young woman and her daughter as family. Was it such an unrealistic expectation? Only time would tell.

Five

When Can I Sing, Mama?

As Max and Hannah sat in the living room, she noted the sprinkling of boyish freckles across Max's nose—freckles that would vanish under the tan that summertime would bring. She went into the kitchen and returned bearing a small glass bowl of blueberries, which she set on the table between their chairs.

"What's going to happen, do you think?" she asked.

"With Miriam and Sadie?"

"Them, too, but I mean with Amelia."

"Amelia's gonna have to deal with them. And she needs to begin by accepting the fact that they didn't have a darn thing to do with the cheating, lying son of a gun her husband turned out to be."

"Amelia needs time," Hannah said. "This is devastating for her. A stranger appears at the door, announces that she's Amelia's husband's daughter by another woman. That's heavy stuff, Max."

"If I hadn't gone over just then and let them in, Amelia

would never have allowed them in the house. That little kid had no gloves or hat. She was freezing out there."

"Whose fault was that? Certainly not Amelia's." Usually critical of Amelia, Hannah now defended her.

"No, of course not, but still, the poor little kid." He took a handful of berries and ate them.

"Under different circumstances, I think they'd like one another. Miriam seems like a nice woman."

"A little mouselike, don't you think?" Max asked. "Jumps at the slightest noise."

"That's exactly how I used to be, when I was married to Bill Parrish. Over time, abusive men brainwash women. We come to believe we're worthless, and that the abuse is not only deserved, but precipitated by something we've said or done, or *not* said or done. At least Miriam had the guts to get out."

Max reached for Hannah's hand and squeezed it gently. "Here." He extended the bowl to her. "These blueberries are sweet. Good for the brain, too, I hear."

Hannah reached for a handful of berries. "In my day, there weren't any shelters to hide in. My parents had both passed away; my brother and I never liked each other very much. I hadn't anyone to turn to for help."

"It must have been terrible. I thought of you yesterday when I was over at your place and heard Miriam's story. I guess that's what prompted me to bring them here."

"You're a good man, Max. I love that you did that."

"I'm sorry I couldn't consult with you first."

"How could you? I wasn't here. We've got four bedrooms,

and have you noticed that Anna thinks Sadie is God's gift? Sadie's taken to her, too. She follows her around like a puppy. It's fine for them to stay as long as they want or need to, as long as it won't intrude on your privacy. I go home most nights now, and you like quiet evenings to read your paper, watch reruns of *Bonanza*, and rest."

"For now it's okay. Let's see how it goes," he said.

"What do you think we should do about Amelia? How do we get them together, so that they can get to know one another? I don't think it's going to just happen."

They were quiet, eating the berries. Then Hannah asked, "Should we invite Amelia over here for dinner, or take them over there to visit?"

"That's a Grace job, I think. Give it a little time, and Grace will help Amelia see that this isn't about Miriam or Sadie. Let's do nothing for now. I know you like things done right away, but you said yourself, it's a big blow for Amelia, a lot for her to digest."

Max shook his head. "So, we'll assume Miriam and Sadie'll be living with us for a while. Lord, but they're gonna think we've got a strange arrangement; we're married, but you live mainly with the ladies across the street."

"The way I see it, that's our business, and Miriam will have to take us as we are," Hannah said.

"And Sadie?" he asked. "What's she gonna think?"

"Whether they stay here or with us ladies over at the house, Sadie will come to understand that you and I are married, and that sometimes I stay at your house and sometimes I stay across the street. Kids take things as they are, so long as they feel safe and people don't lie to them." A worried look crossed her face. "Will they be safe in Covington, do you think, Max?"

"How can we know that? We don't know who Miriam's ex-husband is, what kind of connections or money he's got, or how hell-bent he is on finding them." He stopped, suddenly aware that Hannah was shivering. "You're cold. I should have turned on the heat. Can't get the temperature right in this old house this time of year. It's forty-five degrees in the mornings, warms to seventy-five by the afternoon, then back down to the forties. I'm gonna pick up some space heaters for this room."

She smiled at him. He was so sweet and thoughtful. "Time was, I was a regular Eskimo; loved the cold, loved walking in the snow. Now my legs and knees ache in the cold weather. All of me aches when I get cold. It's just one of those things a person has to learn to deal with as we get older. That storm threw me off. At this time of year, it's usually spring."

"The cows are as confused as you are. Jose and I had a heck of a time rounding up that last cow and her calf."

"Where were they?"

"Up behind that rock outcropping. I guess they went up there to get out of the wind and couldn't find their way out."

They rose, and Max slipped an arm about her shoulders. Hannah leaned against him.

"Let's go on up to bed," he said. His arm about her, they walked upstairs and tiptoed past Miriam and Sadie's room. No light shone under their door.

"They must have been exhausted," Hannah whispered.

• • •

Earlier, while Max and Hannah were chatting in the living room, Miriam had drawn a bath in the large blue and white tile bathroom, and mother and daughter settled into the warm water. Miriam sprinkled in the bubble bath she had picked up at Target earlier. Swishing their hands, they created a froth of bubbles. Sadie giggled and put bubbles on her face and on her mother's to make beards.

"You look funny, Mama, like Mrs. Santa Claus." Sadie lay back against her mother's chest. "I want to live with Mr. Max forever," she whispered, reaching up with her fingers to touch her mother's cheek.

Miriam held her close and silently agreed.

When they stood to shower off the suds, Miriam leaned down and rubbed her nose against her daughter's. "This is how Eskimos in Alaska kiss."

Sadie giggled.

They stepped from the tub, wrapped themselves in big, fluffy bath towels, and dried each other's hair. Once in their new pajamas, they snuggled into the queen-sized bed they shared in the bedroom Hannah called the blue room.

One foot down from the high ceiling, a deep white molding separated the pale blue walls of the room from a dark blue band of color that ran above the molding.

"It's like a river's running around the room." Sadie giggled. "We're sleeping under a river," she sang in a sweet, clear voice.

Miriam had put her fingers to her lips. "Hush, sweetheart. We don't want to disturb anyone."

Sadie pouted. "I'm always having to hush when I want to sing."

Miriam held her close. "I know, Sadie, and I'm sorry. Someday we'll have our own home and a yard, and you can sing as loudly as you want."

"Can I have a dog?"

"Yes. When we have our own home, you can have a dog."

There was a moment of silence. "Will Daddy be there?"

Miriam drew a deep breath. "No."

"Good." Sadie tilted her head up, and trusting blue eyes looked into her mother's. "If he's there, I won't ever be able to sing."

"You'll be able to sing, my little love. I promise you that. You'll be free to run, and play, and sing. What do say we put out the light now? I'll tell you a fairy tale, and we'll see who falls asleep first." Miriam reached over and pulled the chain on the bedside lamp.

Sadie snuggled close. "I like it here, Mama, better than anywhere we ever lived. And I like Max and Hannah. But not that lady who didn't want us to stay in her house."

Miriam kissed her daughter's forehead. "Sometimes it's not a good idea to take someone by surprise. Not everyone likes surprises. Now, shut your eyes. Once upon a time . . ."

Lying in bed, her eyes wide open, Miriam heard Hannah and Max walk past the room. How good and how safe she felt in this house, lying in a soft bed tucked between cool sheets. For a moment she felt as if she'd happened into a secret place where nothing and no one could reach her, but her mind raced with memories.

As a child she had buried herself in Hans Christian Andersen and the Grimm brothers' fairy tales. She had once owned the entire color series of fairy tales: *The Red Fairy Book*, *The Blue Fairy Book*, and so on. Her romance and courtship with Darren had been like a fairy tale, too—except for one incident that, had she been more experienced with men, or had she felt comfortable discussing it with her mother, would have set warning bells ringing.

They had met at a friend's birthday party aboard a chartered ship, drifting down the Thames River. The attraction had been instant, and he had set about wooing her with compliments, champagne, dancing on deck under a full moon. He had phoned the next day, and the next, and for three weeks they had been inseparable.

She took him home to meet her mother, who afterward had compressed her lips, then said, "He seems nice enough, but he's too good-looking, Miriam. Men like that make great lovers and lousy husbands."

But at twenty-two, she had been giddy and insane with love. Ripe for the picking, they would say in America.

His parents, vacationing in France, had invited her and Darren to join them for a weekend in Avignon, a walled city on the banks of the Rhône in Provence. A beautiful city, its narrow, quiet streets were lined with sidewalk cafés and excellent restaurants.

Darren's mother, Althea, loved museums, and they had spent several hours touring the palace's museum of sixteenth-century religious art. His father, Anthony, had suggested attending a play at the world-famous Festival of Avignon, and they had enjoyed a performance of *As You Like It* in English. His parents had been kind to her, gracious, easy to be with.

Darren had proposed, slipping a two-carat diamond on her finger as they sipped wine in a café on the Ile de la Barthelasse in the middle of the Rhône River at sunset. She would always remember the view of the bridge, Pont St-Bénézet, popularly known as the Pont d'Avignon, golden at sunset, its four wide arches reflected in the clear, still river.

It was on that magical weekend that the incident occurred that should have alerted her. At dinner in an elegant restaurant, she had inadvertently spilled red wine on the damask tablecloth. Darren had reached across the table, his eyes steely, and squeezed her hand so hard, she had winced in pain.

"Don't *ever* embarrass me like this again," he had said, his voice hard and cold.

The waiter handled the incident calmly and efficiently, while she had felt incompetent and a perfect fool. Lord, if only she had had the good sense to recognize the cruelty behind the veneer of good looks and sweet talk.

Beside her, Sadie stirred. Miriam looked down at the sleeping child her chest rhythmically rising and falling, a few damp curls clinging to her cheek.

If she hadn't married Darren, she would not have Sadie—and Sadie was worth it all.

Six

RESISTANCE

The unexpected snowfall melted rapidly, and Amelia busied herself with work. Photographing reflections in the river that curved and twisted its way to the hamlet of Pensacola, just north and west of Burnsville, had become her passion. Amelia planned another coffee-table book of seasonal reflections, and this section of the river offered strikingly varied images that continually amazed her.

Two days after the snowstorm, the riverbank was devoid of snow. Amelia lifted her folding chair from the trunk of the car and lugged it down the gently sloping bank. Green with fresh spring grass, the earth was uneven and spongy, and she moved cautiously.

Then, she settled into the chair, her camera bag and equipment close at hand, and waited. If she were patient, the nuances of the river would envelop her and she would enter a slightly altered state of consciousness in which minute shifts and changes revealed themselves. A shimmer of wind might wrinkle the water, blurring a reflection of clearly defined bark and leaves and producing a charming impressionistic effect. A rock protruding serenely above the water could, in the wink of an eye, appear to move, to drift with the current or seem suspended in a whirl of clouds.

But today, as she waited, Amelia's mind floated far away, to France and Thomas, and their glamorous lifestyle.

He had been an important man, a highly successful fundraiser for the International Red Cross. The goal was noble; the more money raised, the more people in disaster areas could be helped with food and shelter.

Socializing with the right people had been of the utmost importance to his work, and they had entertained two or three times a week in their spacious apartment in Paris. The food and drinks were catered; organizing the event and facilitating the smooth flow of the evening fell to her; and Amelia poured her creativity and her energies into the planning of what became highly touted social events.

Thinking back, she realized that Thomas's trips to England had increased in duration—from a day or two, to several days, to a week, to occasionally a week plus the weekend. On several occasions she had suggested joining him, but he had joked about how boring his work was, how wives were not involved, and that the clubs he must go to with potential contributors were as stuffy as the men whom he must court.

"Don't you ever go to the theater? There's wonderful theater in London," she had said, thinking that she would enjoy that, and shopping.

He had pulled her to him and kissed her. Remembering brought tears to her eyes. She had believed that all was well with them and with the world, while all the while he was engaged in an affair.

She gritted her teeth, recalling his words: "I miss you so much when I'm away, but I don't stay long in London these days. I'm out and about in the countryside, mollycoddling chaps with bulging pockets. Sizable donations get them sizable tax write-offs. You understand that."

She had nodded, wanting him to understand that she appreciated how draining his work was. He had lied again and again, and she had accepted his words as true. She'd had no reason to think otherwise.

Calm yourself, Amelia. You'll get no work done today if you let yourself get all riled up like this. Think about what Grace said. There's no self-healing in beating yourself up over the past.

But she couldn't stop remembering, questioning, hating her own gullibility. What had she really known about his working life, other than that he had an office in Paris, a personable, bright young man as his assistant, and an older spinster-type secretary?

Enough of this. Enough!

Amelia unfastened her camera-bag strap and removed her Pentax and the long lens. *As old photographs fade with time, so will all this: the regret, the shame, the hurt. Be glad for all those years you did not know.*

Sunshine struck a round boulder that rose above the waterline. Something moved, capturing her attention. *Rocks don't move. What is it?* Amelia brought the camera to her eye and focused. A snake, camouflaged in several shades of grayish brown to match the boulder, lay sunning itself. She willed the creature to move, to slither down the boulder, to slip into the water stirring ripples, creating a point of interest. The snake remained recumbent. *I could throw a rock.* But why trouble the creature?

Her attention shifted upriver. The late afternoon sunlight played on small rapids that spun the churning water into threads of silver as it rounded the bend. Past the rapids the river grew placid, as reflective as a mirror.

The river worked its spell and Amelia forgot herself as her keen eye spied images that she considered strange, or exciting, or different. After shooting two rolls of film, she set her camera on her lap and quietly watched the water and the snake, indifferent on its perch.

A leaf from a branch above fell into her lap. She smoothed it with her palm, lifted it to the sun and studied the transparency of its veins, its former network of life. Cradling the leaf in her hands, she carried it to the river and laid it on the water, then watched it drift away.

The sun sank lower and the light softened. The trees cast longer shadows across the water. Satisfied with the day's work, Amelia packed up her gear, lugged the chair back up the bank, stashed it and her equipment away, and slid into her car. She checked her watch. She would never make it back to Covington in time for dinner.

As she drove through Burnsville, a sign on a bank bearing the date and time reminded her that today was her birthday. Amelia slapped her forehead with her palm. She had forgotten her own birthday—as had everyone else, it seemed. Several years ago, anticipating turning seventy had been very traumatic. The thought of nonbeing frightened her. Was there really life after death? And if so, what kind of life would it be?

There were no answers, of course; not for her or the millions of others who had asked such questions. Faith helped. Her father had had that kind of blind faith. He believed in good and evil, God versus the devil, the fires of hell. As an adult, meeting people of different religious beliefs in the Sudan, in India, in Italy, the Netherlands, and in Israel and France, Amelia came to believe that it was how a person lived, rather than what religious denomination they claimed as their own, that mattered most. She found it interesting that concepts of an afterlife differed.

She had never given reincarnation any thought until she lived in India. And now that she was on the shorter end of her life, it hardly seemed logical that the accumulated knowledge of a lifetime should go to waste. The concept of reincarnation had become much more appealing.

What might she feel if she made it to eighty? Would she be more or less afraid of dying? And what about ninety? Recently she had photographed several ninety-year-old women, cousins who lived close by one another along a river in a cove in Yancy County. Lucille managed, with arthritic fingers, to make corncob dolls. Squinting over the thread, Mary Alice quilted by hand, while Mattie knitted shawls. Every holiday season, these ladies donated their year's work to their church's community center fund-raiser.

"I'm gonna knit you a cap for winter. It'll just take me a

while. I work a heap slower these days," Miss Mattie said when Amelia last visited her. Amelia wanted to ask Mattie how she felt about dying, but of course she had not done so.

When Amelia arrived home, cars lined Cove Road and jammed Max's driveway. There was scarcely room to pull her car into her own driveway. Lights brightened every window of the house, and a sense of expectation rushed through her as she lugged her equipment up the steps.

The front door flew open. "Surprise!" everyone yelled. Arms reached out to hug her. Someone took the camera bag and tripod. "Happy birthday, Amelia!"

A warm glow filled her. Grace and Bob, Hannah and Max, Hannah's daughter Laura and her husband Hank were there. And Brenda was there, and her daughter Molly, and her husband Ted, and eighty-seven-year old Lurina, smelling of mothballs from a dress that had been stored for special occasions. Mike, her former photography instructor and good friend, was grinning like a Cheshire cat. He'd known and never said a word. Balloons floated close to the ceiling, and the homey, welcoming smell of baking lingered in the air.

Grace stepped forward to hug her. "We were so worried about you. Where were you?"

"I'm sorry. I was at the river in Burnsville, and the time flew by. I forgot it was my birthday. Thank you all for remembering."

"When you didn't come, we started eating dinner, a buffet. There's plenty. Come and sit and I'll get you a plate," Grace said.

"I need to wash up. Let me run upstairs and change." As she turned, Amelia spotted Miriam standing in the kitchen doorway. She wore one of Grace's aprons, and seemed as comfortable as if she had been there for years. Abruptly, Amelia's mood shifted. Rationality flew out the window and feelings of anger, resentment, and shame raced through her. She wanted that woman and her child out of this house this very instant!

"What's she doing here?" Amelia hissed.

"Come on, Amelia. Miriam's staying at Max's place. We couldn't ignore her and Sadie. Forget them, stay calm, and focus on your celebration." Grace slipped an arm about Amelia and walked her toward the stairs. "You run on up and change, then we'll celebrate your birthday. The kids have a big surprise for you. They've been on pins and needles waiting for you. Come on, now." She nudged Amelia onto the first step and looked at her pointedly. "You can do this."

As she washed her face and brushed her teeth, Amelia heard the happy voices from below and her resentment soared. How could Grace and Hannah do this to her? She'd said she needed time, and they weren't allowing her time. Amelia banged her hairbrush so hard against the side of the sink that the plastic handle broke into two sections and scattered on the bathroom floor. She ignored them, and put on her makeup, focusing on the children waiting below to give her their presents. Later, she would give Grace a good piece of her mind.

At the foot of the stairs, Grace and Hannah hooked their arms through hers and guided her into the living room, where everyone stood in a semicircle, looking at her.

Calm down, Amelia, she told herself. *You can ruin this party for everyone, or you can relax and enjoy it. Snubbing Miriam might give them sympathy for the woman. But what about me? Where's their sympathy for me? Stop it! Smile. Walk into that room and be gracious.* Amelia lifted her head, threw back her shoulders, and allowed Hannah and Grace to lead her to a chair.

Bob's grandson Tyler, a teenager now, prodded his sister, Melissa, and Hannah's little grandson, Andy, toward Amelia. With Tyler's help, he walked toward her carrying a big box.

"Happy birthday, Aunt Amelia," Tyler said. "We got this special present for you." The children looked at her expectantly, their eyes shining. "We hope you like it."

Andy climbed onto Amelia's lap. "Open your present," he said. She let him untie the ribbon and tear off the wrappings. Tyler opened the box, and Melissa reached inside and drew out two handfuls of film cartons: print film, slide film, black-and-white film.

"I wanna give Auntie Amelia film," Andy said.

"And you shall," Amelia said, tipping the box so he could reach inside. That done, Amelia embraced them. "What a wonderful present this is. I love it. I'll take pictures of each and every one of you with the very first roll I put into my camera."

Someone brought her a plate of ham, sweet potato pudding, corn pudding, and green beans. Suddenly hungry, she ate with gusto, enjoying everything on the plate as her friends moved about the room, sat cross-legged on the carpet, or stood in small clusters near the fireplace or by the windows chatting.

Andy skipped about the room following Melissa, who sang loudly, "Aunt Amelia's gonna take my picture. Goody, goody."

Miriam stood in the foyer, out of Amelia's line of vision. She had argued against coming here today, but Max and Hannah had insisted.

Sadie slipped her hand into her mother's. "They let those kids sing loud in the house, Mama."

"Indeed they do, and they're very loud, too."

Sadie tugged at her hand. "I want to sing. I want to celebrate the party, too."

"Not just yet, my love."

"This party was a surprise for Amelia, and she's not mad. You said she didn't like surprises," Sadie said.

Miriam kneeled beside her daughter and held her close. "These children have known Amelia for years. We're strangers. That's the difference."

"How long does it take to not be a stranger?"

"Sometimes not very long; sometimes it takes a very long time." Miriam stood. "Come, Grace is cutting the cake. All the layers are different colors. It's called a Vienna cake. See how pretty it is? Let's go have some."

Amelia turned her attention to Brenda, who was talking about Hannah's work with the garden club at Caster Elementary School, where Brenda was the principal.

"She's absolutely marvelous with the children," Brenda

said to Mike. "We have at least two dozen budding young horticulturists."

Amelia rose and moved to where Molly and Laura were deep in conversation with Max; the young women worked for Max at Bella's Park. Their jobs included researching and obtaining authentic furnishings and clothing for the Covington homesteads, part of a living museum at the park.

"We can't find them," Molly said. "We have only pictures of them."

"They must be available somewhere. If not in Madison County, then in Tennessee, maybe," Max said.

"What are you looking for?" Amelia asked.

Molly brushed her long, dark hair back from her face. "House slippers. We'd like to set a pair by one of the beds in the Covington Homestead, but slippers from the late eighteen hundreds didn't last, unlike a cooking pot or a farm tool."

"Well, you could have them made, if need be, I have the name of a woman who sews Victorian and other costumes for parties," Amelia said.

"Oh, do give me her name," Molly said.

"I'll find it tomorrow and call you." Amelia circled the room, chatting with this person and that. Out of the corner of her eye, she saw Grace take Sadie's hand and lead her to where Andy and Melissa played with a box of dominoes. They stacked them and lined them in rows. Suddenly Andy, obviously angry with Melissa, stood and kicked the dominoes, scattering them about the room. Melissa shrieked at the top of her lungs, stopping all adult conversation. Quietly, without seeking anyone's approval, Sadie picked up the dominoes and one by one handed them to Melissa, who instantly grew quiet.

Is Sadie naturally cooperative, rather than competitive like Andy and Melissa? Interesting. Young as they were, Amelia speculated, they already exhibited distinct character traits—and she thought about how abilities one was born with could be cultivated or stifled, as hers had been.

When she was nine, she had spent an afternoon on the beach, sitting with her back against hard, dark rocks near the shore, out of sight of their home on the bluff above. One of her long braids hung down across her chest, while the other trailed down her back. Amelia could see her face, small, pixielike, intent, the tip of her tongue protruding slightly from between her lips.

Her mother's oil paints had been forbidden to her, and she had sneaked a pad, brushes, and several tubes of paint she had chosen for their names, rather than for her knowledge of their colors: cerulean blue, russet, magenta, forest green. Her ocean waves, drawn with ragged wavy lines, and the smears she called trees standing on what she considered to be the seashore, had they been a little bit good? Had she exhibited the tiniest bit of talent?

Her mother, her face red with rage, had torn the pad from Amelia's hands and tossed it into the trash, and she had suffered a sound spanking and been exiled to her room for daring to touch those paints. The pain in her heart had far overshadowed the pain to her legs and buttocks. Deeply crushed, Amelia vowed never to pick up a paintbrush again, and she never had.

Looking back, it was clear to her that all her life, she had squelched her own interests and skills. She had lived her husband's agenda, telling herself that his work was important and valuable, and served mankind. Which it did. But she had lost herself in the process, and when Thomas died, there was nothing—no sense of self, of who she was, of anything that she had accomplished.

Her eyes met Grace's, and they smiled at one another. Grace and Hannah's friendship, their tolerance and acceptance of her, had freed her to pick up a camera and take lessons from Mike, with wondrous results. If, as Grace believed, everything in life prepared a person for the future, then all those years of living with Thomas had not been in vain. Something inside of her had been taking root, preparing for her to grow and blossom into the person, the photographer, she was today. Was she now also a big enough person to accept Miriam and Sadie, regardless of how angry and hurt she was?

Melissa and Sadie laughed, and their gay, light laughter drew her back to her birthday party. Amelia closed her eyes and let the love around her give her the joy it was intended to give. When she opened her eyes, Miriam came into view, moving about the room, clearing glasses, stopping to talk to Lurina.

What were Miriam's skills and talents? she wondered. She had been a teacher; had she enjoyed it? What if Brenda offered her a job at her school? Would she stay in Covington? Nonsense, what was there for a young woman in Covington?

She thought of Stella. How had she earned a living if Thomas had not supported her, as Miriam had implied?

Amelia gazed at Sadie, watching how kind the little girl was to Melissa, who had grown calm in her presence. *Lord, but that child looks like my Caroline. So many years, and any reminder of Caroline still has the power to make me sad.* When Sadie turned their eyes met and held, and the child smiled. For a moment, Amelia's heart melted—then she looked away.

Seven

Wanting to Belong

On a sunny Sunday morning after Amelia's birthday, Miriam sat in the living room with Max and Hannah. Anna and Jose had asked to take Sadie to visit a cousin of Anna's, who had a granddaughter Sadie's age.

"You no worry about nothing, Señora Miriam," Jose said. "We take good care of Sadie, like she's our own granddaughter."

"Please, Mama, let me go. I'll be fine." Sadie held Anna's hand.

"*Sí,*" Anna looked at Sadie and smiled. She laid her hand on Sadie's head. "*La quiero mucho a ella.*"

And Miriam, seeing the caring in Anna's eyes, hearing it in her voice, although still uncertain, agreed.

The bell on Cove Road Church rang, heralding the Sunday morning service. Miriam went to the low, wide windows and watched people arrive, then she turned from the window and rejoined Max and Hannah.

"You were going to tell us about your life, my dear," Hannah said. "Seems a good time, with Sadie away visiting."

Miriam sank into a chair beside Hannah. Bit by bit, occasionally stopping to wipe away tears, she poured out her story.

"We were married in England. It was a very small wedding. His parents did not come to England. His mother, Althea, wrote that it was too much of a trip for his father, considering that we had all met when they were vacationing a few months earlier in France. His father had contracted some kind of virus on that trip and still wasn't up to a long plane journey. So mainly friends of my mine and my mother's attended our wedding.

"In the weeks prior to the wedding, Darren was especially solicitous of my mother." Miriam's brows drew together. "He had these moods. You never knew how he would be."

"What kind of moods?" Hannah asked.

"For periods of time he would be very upbeat, then he would grow morose and irritable. I think they call it bipolar, but I'd never heard that word until I was watching television after Sadie was born. I think Darren had it, and it got worse with time."

She straightened her shoulders. "Weddings are stressful, and I chose to overlook Darren's behavior—especially because he was most often pleasant with my mother, and I could see that she had set aside her reservations about him, which pleased me. Looking back, I believe Darren treated her this way deliberately. It was his way of setting me up, you might say. After we were married, my mother refused to believe anything negative I said about Darren. But then . . ."

Miriam hesitated. "Finally, when she was ill, and I explained my life with him without telling her the worst of it, she must have realized. For she told me about my father and gave me his address and said to use it only in the most dire of circumstances. Strange words, don't you think?"

"She may have had a sixth sense," Hannah said.

"The abuse started when we moved to America, only I hadn't a name for what was going on. You know how a couple might joke with one another, roughhouse a bit?"

Max and Hannah exchanged a quick glance. "No, I'm afraid I don't quite know what you mean," Max said.

"He'd turn rough when I least expected it. I'd push him away and tell him he was hurting me. Straightaway, he'd apologize. But he'd soon be doing it again.

"I was five months pregnant with Sadie when the first serious incident occurred. I'd bought a maternity dress, one of those loose-fitting ones with a Hawaiian print. We were to have dinner with his parents. He yelled at me, 'You can't wear that piece of crap to my parents' home,' and literally tore the dress off me—right there in the open doorway. I was mortified, as you can imagine."

Hannah reached over and patted her hand. "That must have been humiliating. Miriam, if it troubles you to tell us this, then don't. Max, dear, will you get her a glass of water?"

He rose and returned with a glass, setting it on a cork coaster on the small round table between their chairs.

Miriam nodded her thanks, drank, and continued. "I do want to tell you. I trust you. Well, after that, it seemed that nothing I did, or was, pleased him. I was too fat. My legs were barrels. He hated my hair, said it was dull and had lost its sheen, and he couldn't stand to touch it, or me. I'd lost my looks, and on and on. By the time Sadie was born, I was a mess—a weepy sponge soaking up the verbal abuse he heaped on me, losing confidence, hating myself.

"At one point after she was born, I wasn't even sure I was competent enough to take care of Sadie. There was a woman whom I met in a nearby park, where I'd take the baby in those first few months before he forbade me to go to the park. Sadie could catch a disease, he said. People were so dirty. Anyway, that woman spoke kindly to me. She said I handled the baby beautifully and was a natural mother. I'll always remember her with gratitude. Her kind words literally saved my sanity."

Miriam looked from Max to Hannah. "My mother believed that we all have guardian angels. I've often thought that the woman in the park was mine. I never saw her again, though there were times I'd sneak out to the park to find her, to thank her."

Incident after incident, one more appalling than the other, poured out of Miriam. Darren had sold her car and denied her access to his car. It enraged him if she talked to another woman, or invited a friend over. She had been forbidden to chat on the phone with other women, or to shop for clothes by herself. She was incompetent to choose stylish clothing, he said. His unpredictability unnerved her, terrified her, and she had walked on egg shells.

Remembering her own life with Bill Parrish, Hannah empathized with everything Miriam said.

Miriam told them how his blows were aimed away from her face and fell short of breaking bones, precluding the need to go to the hospital. "I had no one to confide in, no way out. If not for Sadie, I would have gone mad," she said. "Then one day, I saw an ad on the television about abuse—the emotional kind as well as the physical—and I finally acknowledged that I was one of them. An abused woman. Somehow, then, I garnered the courage to punch that number into the phone." She sighed deeply. "And that act brought the help that I needed."

Hannah wiped tears from her eyes. "Miriam, I lived with a man like your husband. I know what it does to you."

Miriam's eyed widened. "You were abused? How is that possible? Surely not you."

Hannah nodded. "Yes, me. It could be any one of us. You were brave to seek help and to divorce him. In my day, there was no place to turn. I stayed until it got so bad that one night I finally threw my girls into the car and fled. A stranger helped me and I got away from him, but I had to hide. Like you, I was terrified he would come after us. He was a hunter, and guns were all over the house. Lucky for me, he died of a stroke soon after—undoubtedly brought on by his explosive rages. Otherwise he would surely have found us, and God only knows what would have happened."

"If only that would happen to Darren, a stroke or an accident, anything! Just die and leave us in peace." She clapped her hands over her mouth. "I know it's wrong to even think that, but I just don't know how else I'll ever be free of him. He's a determined man and patient. He threatened to kill us, and I believe he would if he could. I'm so afraid he'll find us," she whispered.

That was Hannah's and Max's fear, as well.

Hannah's eyes held Miriam's. "I doubt he'll find you here. And we will do everything we can to protect you."

"I cannot thank you enough for everything you've done for Sadie and me. You've taken us in and cared for us. I bless you with all my heart."

Outside, activity stirred. Women returned to their cars after church holding their skirts and hats against the wind. Car doors slammed. Engines started. A horn blew, and cars began to leave Cove Road.

Moments later, the doorbell rang, and Miriam jumped. Fear filled her eyes, and she half rose from her chair.

Max went to the window. "It's okay, Miriam. It's only Grace's son Roger."

Pale and trembling, Miriam sank back into the chair.

Hannah opened the door, admitting a tall, nice-looking, middle-aged man who hugged her.

Max said, "Roger lives in South Carolina, way out in the country." The two men hugged one another, and Miriam was impressed by the warmth between them.

Roger grinned. "Well, well, if this isn't the height of domesticity. I thought you lived over yonder, Hannah?" He nodded toward the ladies' house across the street.

"I'm like a jack-in-the-box." Hannah laughed. "Now you see me, now you don't. How are you, Roger? You up for a visit? Your mother didn't say you were coming."

"A spur-of-the-moment decision. I haven't seen you all in

months. I figured I'd surprise her, but Mother isn't home and neither is Amelia."

"They're seeing a play in Asheville this afternoon."

"Sit, Roger. Can I get you a drink?" Max asked.

"Oh, goodness, my manners." Hannah slipped her arm around Miriam, gathering her in. "This is Miriam Declose-Smith. She's staying with us."

Roger stepped forward and hugged Miriam. "Any relative of Amelia's is a relative of mine."

"Oh, no. I'm not a relative of Amelia's."

"It's a long story, Roger," Max said. "I'll let Miriam tell you whatever part of it she chooses to."

"Are you hungry?" Hannah asked.

"I'm starved." Roger slipped off his jacket, set it on a straight-backed chair against the wall, unknotted his tie and let it hang loose. "I'm glad church is out, otherwise I never would have found a place to park. How come there are so many cars? I can't remember it being like this."

"It's Denny Ledbetter, the young pastor who came to help Pastor Johnson. People like him and his sermons—they're short and to the point," Max said.

"There's leftover stew and strawberry pie that Anna made," Hannah said. "You talk with Max, and I'll rustle you up some dinner."

"I'll help you." Miriam hastened after Hannah.

"Miriam looked scared to death when I hugged her. What's her problem?" Roger took Hannah's chair near Max. He stretched his long legs, eased off his shoes, and rubbed the soles of his feet with his toes. "Darn shoes are too tight. I wear mainly moccasins these days, and when I put on lace-up shoes or boots, they feel like vises." He nodded toward the kitchen. "So, who is Miriam?"

Max lowered his voice. "She's the daughter of Amelia's husband Thomas, by some woman in England."

Roger gave a low whistle. "You gotta be kidding."

"No. They arrived here last week out of the blue. Hell of a shock for Amelia. She refused to have anything to do with them, refused to let them stay with her."

"Who's them?"

"Miriam has a little girl. The dearest child you ever met, pretty and sweet-natured. She's seven. Anna and Jose took her with them to visit relatives. Hannah thinks Amelia will soften with time. She and Grace have this idea that Miriam and Sadie will turn out to be the family Amelia doesn't have."

Roger whistled softly again. "Something's always happening with you guys."

"We're like a tribe, and what affects one affects us all." The men laughed. "Tell me, how's it going with you?" Max asked.

"Good, really good. I've bought a small tractor and plowed the field by the river. This year I'm putting in corn, beans, peppers, and potatoes," Roger said. "Now don't you go laughing at me, but I've taken up baking bread. I brought a couple of loaves for everyone. The best bread you'll ever taste. As soon as the tailgate markets in Salem, Walhalla, Seneca, and Westminster start up in May, I'll be selling it there."

"Bread. Well, that's a new one. But why not? You'll be a huge success, I'm sure," Max said.

"I find baking bread amazingly relaxing," Roger said. "The smell reminds me of when I was a child and my mother baked."

"Funny, isn't it, how as we get older we're attracted to smells, places, things from our past? Hannah's been on a campaign to locate a mahogany sideboard with a mirror attached, like one in her mother's dining room when she was a kid. Thank God she's got Amelia and Grace, and now Miriam to run around to antique stores with, or she'd have me in tow."

"So, tell me about this Miriam. Is she here to stay?"

Max sighed. "Hard to tell. She's on the run from an abusive man she divorced, who's threatened to kill her and Sadie. Hell of a thing."

"How terrible. She must be so frightened and so brave, the poor thing. You worried he'll find her?"

Max nodded. At that moment the women returned, Hannah carrying a tray with a bowl of steaming hot stew, and Miriam with the pie and four plates.

"Here we are. You just sit right here by the window and eat this, Roger." Hannah handed him the tray. "Then we'll all have a piece of Anna's pie with whipped cream."

Roger steadied the tray on his lap and began to eat, blowing on each spoonful as he brought it to his lips. "It's good. Thanks a heap."

"Roger's baking bread these days, and he's brought us all loaves. He's gonna sell it at the tailgate markets around

Salem and Walhalla," Max said. "Before you know it, he'll be the bread king of Oconee County, South Carolina."

"Wonderful," Hannah said. "When you're done with that stew, Roger, bring us in your bread. I'll get the butter and sample it."

Max laughed. "The way this is going, we'll be eating all night."

Miriam felt herself drawn into the warmth of this extended family circle, some of whom she had met at Amelia's birthday party. Several, she had learned, worked together in one capacity or another. Grace and Hannah volunteered with kids at Brenda's school. Hannah had organized a young people's garden club, and it was those kids who had planted and now tended the Children's Garden at Bella's Park. Grace was, for all intents and purposes, grandmother to Bob's grandchildren, though they were not related, even by marriage. Mike and Amelia seemed as comfortable with one another as happily married people, only Mike was gay. And Miss Lurina, who looked to be a hundred years old, treated Grace as if she were her daughter. They were extraordinary people who loved one another, and in this short time, she had come to like, admire, and respect them.

Suddenly, what Miriam wanted more than anything in the world was to be accepted by Amelia, to become a part of this wonderful, warm surrogate family. She would do anything if Amelia would only give her a chance.

Eight

Amelia Vacillates

Amelia enjoyed the play that she and Grace attended at the Asheville Community Theater. Grace, prone to what Amelia considered an excess of sentimentality, sniffed back tears and blew her nose throughout. During the intermission Amelia suggested that they leave, but Grace, her eyes red and puffy, shook her head. "It's all right. I'm enjoying the play, and a good cry doesn't hurt anyone."

"Why would anyone want to cry, if they don't have to?" Amelia asked her later, as they drove to the restaurant for an early dinner. She thought of the night she had gone to Grace's room to chat and found her friend teary-eyed and sniffling over some novel she was reading.

"It's cathartic," Grace replied. "I've always cried at weddings, even strangers' weddings on TV or in a movie." She tilted her head. "And then I get over it."

They ate at T.K. Tripps Restaurant in Asheville, sitting in a booth beside a large window. Tall shrubs outside obscured the passing traffic, and on the hillside beyond, lights twinkled in homes tucked among the trees.

They placed their orders. Then Grace said, "I want to talk to you."

"What about?" Amelia lifted her spoon and dangled it over her water glass.

"About Miriam."

Amelia looked out of the window. "I thought we agreed that I would take my time figuring out what to do about her. What if I don't want to talk about Miriam right this minute?"

"When, then? It's been a while since we discussed her."

Amelia's lower lip quivered. "Maybe I need several months, or even a year. Who are you, or anyone, to decide when I've gotten over being hurt and humiliated?"

"There's a time for everything, and you're clinging to foolish pride. Look, Amelia." Grace leaned forward and her voice grew soft. "The one thing Hannah and I have that you don't have is a family. Oh, I know we all have a wonderful surrogate family, whom we love. But here's this woman and child, and they're all alone with no one in the world. What if Thomas had had an early marriage and Miriam was your stepdaughter? Couldn't you think of her that way? I see how your eyes soften when you look at Sadie, and your voice, too, when you speak about her. She's a lovely little girl. Who wouldn't want a granddaughter like that? Think about it."

Grace paused to drink from her water glass. "Surely it wasn't easy for Miriam to come here to ask for your help. She risked exactly what happened: rejection. If not for Max, where would she have gone that night?"

"She should have written and given me time to get over the shock, not just show up like that. How could she think that I'd welcome her with open arms?" Amelia's spoon struck the rim of the glass.

"Oh, put that spoon down, will you?" Grace said.

Amelia set the spoon on the table. "What's with you, anyway? First you whimper through a play, and now you're cranky."

"I want you to behave like the woman I know you are: generous of spirit and loving."

"It's so hard." Amelia's shoulders slumped. "And even if I wanted to, where would I begin? I've been so adamant."

"That's just pride talking. What if you get together with Miriam in some informal way, get to know her better, break the ice?"

"I guess I could do that," Amelia said. "How?"

"I want to invite Miriam for dinner, and I'd like it very much if you were there. Will you do that for me? Just give her a chance, that's all."

Amelia grunted something.

Their dinners arrived, and they spoke no more about Miriam. When they finished and paid their bill, they started back to Covington. In the car, Grace asked, "So, will you be home for dinner when I ask Miriam?"

Amelia waved her hands. "Okay, stop nagging me. I'll be there."

As they entered Cove Road, Grace's voice rose with excitement. "That's Roger's SUV in Max's driveway."

"Did you expect him this weekend?" Amelia turned the car into Max's drive. "I see him in the window. Look, he's waving. Go on in."

"Aren't you coming?" Grace's door stood half-open. "Come in with me, Amelia."

"No, I think not. Not tonight."

"Please."

"Don't pressure me, Grace."

"Okay." Grace ran from the car and up the steps to where her son stood in the doorway.

Amelia reversed the car and pulled into their driveway across the street. She just wasn't ready to open her arms to Miriam. What would she say at Grace's dinner party? Would she be expected to apologize? Why should she? *She* was the injured party. Well, she'd worry about it all another day. Tonight, she was exhausted.

Inside, Amelia pulled down the shade to avoid the temptation of looking at them through the brightly lit windows of Max's living room.

Later, Roger came home with his mother and settled into the ladies' guest room. As the days passed, he spent most of his time with Miriam and Sadie. They never stopped talking about one thing or another. It was as if he'd known her forever, as if she was a long-lost relative. And Sadie was a sheer delight.

One day, Grace stood in the doorway of Roger's room. "I've hardly seen you since you got here. I want to talk with you, to hear about your life in Salem. Have you gotten your garden in? Down there, you can plant a month earlier than we can, isn't that right?"

Roger stood before the dresser mirror and adjusted his tie. "Yes. It gets warmer weeks earlier."

"Are you happy? What do you do for entertainment? Do you see much of your friend, what was his name, Lennie?"

"Yes, Lennie."

"He seemed like a nice person and is very smart, Hannah says."

"That's right. He teaches at Clemson University. I've taken several horticulture classes from him and learned a great deal."

"There's so much I'd like to ask you, to talk about." Grace barred his way out of the door.

He stood looking down at her. "I'm sorry, Mother. I've been caught up with Miriam and Sadie. They're pretty much alone, you know; everyone works or is busy. I like Miriam, it's as if we're old chums. I know you'd want me to be nice to her."

"I certainly do, and I'm glad you're showing her about. You're right—none of us really has the time to take her around. Until you came, she pretty much hung around Max's house and Bella's Park." Grace stepped sideways, allowing him to leave the room, but she followed him to the front door. "We can only hope that husband of hers doesn't find her."

She grabbed Roger's arm, anxiety in her eyes, and pressed her hand to her chest. "My Lord, Roger, we'd all be in danger, wouldn't we? If he came and he had a gun, I mean."

Maybe Miriam and Sadie ought to come down and stay with me, Roger thought. *I've gotten to know the sheriff and his boys down in Salem, and I could tell them the situation. They'd swing by my house regularly and keep their ears and eyes open. If her ex came snooping about, there's no place around Salem for him to hide. I'll mention it to Miriam and give her my phone numbers.*

"He's not going to find Miriam. Now stop worrying, Mother. It's going to be all right. We're going down to Marshall today. I bet Sadie will get a kick out of the island in the river, where the kids from that area used to go to school. I'd take Melissa with us, but she's such a brat." He was out the door and going down the steps, and still Grace followed him.

"She's been a difficult child from day one," Grace said. "She'd have enjoyed being with Sadie, though. She's crazy about her, and Sadie's so patient with her."

"I guess Melissa's behavior's been exacerbated by her parents' divorce and her mother moving back to Florida. You ever hear from Emily?" He headed toward his car.

Grace walked a step behind him. "Not often. Once a month or so she calls me to ask about Melissa. I guess she and Russell would rather not talk to one another."

"You still taking Melissa to a counselor?" he asked, opening the car door.

Grace grabbed it and held it ajar.

"Would you like to come with us, Mother? We could continue our conversation in the car, and you're welcome to come. We'd all be more comfortable. I know I would," Roger said.

"I'm due at Caster Elementary School in an hour. The little girl I've been tutoring is in a pageant, and I want to be there. You go ahead. Have a good time."

"See you later, then. I'll be back before dinnertime."

Grace watched as he backed out of the driveway and turned into Max's driveway. She watched from their porch as Sadie leaped from a chair on Max's front porch, where she and her mother had been waiting, and flung herself into Roger's arms. He lifted her high into the air, and Grace could hear her squeals of delight. She felt a pang, then—the old pang of regret that Roger would never marry and have children. Then Miriam, Sadie, and Roger climbed into his SUV and drove away.

Grace went inside into the kitchen, where she poured herself a cup of good strong tea. Roger had raised the issue of Melissa, and now she could not get the child out of her mind.

With Russell's approval, she had taken Melissa to a female children's therapist in Asheville, who had helped Melissa a great deal. Playing with dolls and toys and finger paints, Melissa had begun to express her anger at her mother and her father, whom she somehow blamed for her mother leaving. But the child certainly hadn't learned much about managing that anger outside of the therapist's office. Melissa still had rages, screaming and kicking out at things and people. Not as often, though, which offered hope, and Sadie clearly had a salutary effect on Melissa. The child was less irascible around Sadie. To test her theory, Grace had decided to take the girls to a restaurant in Asheville for lunch to see how Melissa would behave with Sadie present.

"You're going to do what? Melissa's a monster in a restaurant. You sure you want to risk that?" Bob had asked, when she told him.

"I want to test my idea."

"At Amelia's party, Melissa had never seen Sadie before. Maybe it was a one-time fluke."

Grace decided to ignore him and proceed with her plan, which was delayed when Roger extended his stay in Covington for another week.

A few days later, Grace once again stood in the doorway of her son's room, her hands on her hips, and watched Roger plop onto the bed, remove his loafers, pull on high-top boots, and begin to lace them. He looked up at her.

"I haven't seen you much this whole trip. When will you have time for us to sit and have a chat?"

He finished tying the laces on his second boot. "Sunday, I promise. I won't make any plans except to be with you. We'll go out for brunch or lunch. How's that?" He smiled at her and her heart softened.

Roger stood. "There! Well, I'm off now. Miriam, Sadie, and I are going horseback riding."

"For heaven's sake, be careful."

"It's a trail ride. These horses plod along a trail in the woods led by a guide. We'll start in Barnardsville and take the trail up into Pisgah Forest. There's a waterfall at the top of the trail, just under the Blue Ridge Parkway. They say it's beautiful and well worth the trip."

"You can get to the Blue Ridge Parkway from there?" Grace rarely traveled on the parkway, except as a shortcut around Asheville south to Biltmore Avenue, and that was only on those rare occasions when she shopped at Harris Teeter Market or picked up dinner at Boston Market. She liked their meat loaf.

"No, you can see the parkway and hear the cars going by, but you can't get to it that way. Now, don't you worry about us. I guarantee, it's a slow, safe ride." He stood and smiled. "Friday night we're going to the Depot in Marshall. You and Bob want to come?"

"What's the Depot?"

"The old train depot. It's been completely renovated, turned into a kind of music hall. They've redone the place: air-conditioned it, put in new seats, and they serve food, though it's not a place you go for dinner. Every Friday night they have a variety show." He pulled on a lightweight jacket. "There's a small stage if anyone gets the urge to get up and dance. This Friday night, they have a country music band and a gospel group from a church. Miriam and I are going, and we'd like it if you and Bob came along."

"I'll ask Bob. How about asking Amelia and Mike to join us?"

"I thought Amelia wasn't having anything to do with Miriam."

Grace followed her son from the bedroom. "Well, it's about time she did. Maybe this could help break the ice. Roger, you will be careful about the horses, won't you? They're such big creatures. Do they kick, do you think?"

He bent and kissed her cheek. "I'll be careful, and no, these horses are very gentle. They won't kick."

Later that day, when Hannah came home, she and Grace sat in the kitchen over cups of tea.

"What's going on with Roger and Miriam, do you think?" Hannah asked. "He spends a lot of time with her and Sadie."

"He sympathizes with Miriam. He says they instantly felt as if they were old friends," Grace said. After Roger left, she'd baked enough sugar cookies to fill their piggy cookie jar plus an equal amount to send to Max's house.

Hannah wiped a smear of flour from Grace's face. "What did you do, jump in the flour?"

"I like to use my hands to mix the ingredients."

"I've never seen Amelia so stubborn." Hannah's brows furrowed, forming a crease above her nose.

Hannah doesn't look seventy-seven years old, Grace thought. *Do I look seventy-four? Hannah has more lines along her cheeks and across her forehead than either Amelia or I do, but I probably have the most cellulite on my thighs. Well, everyone ages differently. Better to focus on coming to terms with the changes, like letting go of those things I can't do or eat anymore, like sugar cookies. Lord, I miss sweets, all kinds of sweets.*

"I'm taking up something new," she told Hannah. "I signed up in Asheville for a class in Scrapbooking."

"Why?"

"It's a substitute for food. It'll keep me busy and my mind off all those sweet things I love."

"It must be hard, this diabetes, having to be so careful about weight and what you eat," Hannah said.

"It is sometimes. Sometimes I'm okay, and I have myself under control. But there are times when I just crave coffee ice cream. Every now and then I buy a pint and devour it all in one sitting. That's really terrible for me, yet I still do it. And I'm so guilty afterward."

The tinfoil mounded about the cookies that Grace stuffed

into a round tin pan. "These are ready to go." Reaching into the piggy jar, she pulled out a cookie.

"What are you doing?" Hannah asked. "What about your diabetes, didn't you just say—"

"I've lost more weight." Grace folded her hands across her chest. "My blood pressure is down, and the doctor's pleased with the way my sugar is lower and more stable. There are times when a person just *has* to have a taste of something they used to love. But I'll only eat one, I promise."

"I just don't know about you, Grace."

"Well, don't you worry. I know how serious diabetes is, but one cookie won't kill me. Not when all the other factors are so stable."

"You're sure of that?"

Disgusted, Grace dumped the cookie back into the jar. "No, darn it. I'm not sure. I probably shouldn't *ever* put this kind of thing into my mouth. I can't make them any more, Hannah. It's torture just to smell them baking."

Hannah sighed and leaned back in the chair. "Then don't. We love them but we love you far more than we do the cookies. And, believe me, we could all do with less sugar."

The cookie jar slid toward Hannah. "Take them all to Max's, will you, please?"

"Good girl. I'm proud of you." Then, Hannah said, "Funny isn't it, how our lives have become consumed with Amelia, Miriam, and her daughter. We talk about them over breakfast and dinner when Amelia's not here, and we worry about things like Miriam's ex-husband showing up. Amelia's still not ready to open her heart; she keeps transferring her anger from that rotten Thomas to Miriam. What do you think we should do?"

"That day we went to the play in Asheville, the day Roger arrived, Amelia agreed to have dinner with Miriam. You and Max come. I'll make Roger's favorite, meatballs with prunes."

"Great idea. Let me know what you want me to do to help." Hannah rose, the cookie jar under one arm, the pan of cookies in the other. "Open the door for me, will you? Miriam and Sadie will enjoy these cookies, as will Anna and Jose, I'm sure, and Max, too."

"Give plenty of them to Jose and Anna."

Hannah nodded. "I'll be home early this evening. I'm going to take a hot bath and get into bed with a good book. And Grace, I'm glad you were able to get Amelia to agree to have dinner with Miriam. It's high time."

Grace closed the front door behind Hannah. With Roger away for the afternoon, she went into the guest room, her favorite spot to relax and watch TV. Roger's bed had been sloppily made, and she straightened the covers, then fluffed and propped the pillows. She picked up Roger's shirt, tossed haphazardly on the back of the rocking chair, sniffed it, determined that it was clean, and hung it in the closet. Then she settled into the rocker and turned on the House and Garden channel.

Designers Challenge was on. Grace enjoyed the presentations made to the homeowner by three different designers. She listened to each presentation carefully, selected one, and muted the commercials as she waited for the third segment, where she would learn of the homeowner's decision. If they were on the same wavelength and selected the same designer, Grace clapped her hands with pleasure. Now, these were smart people! When they chose a different designer, she frowned and informed the TV characters that they had made a huge mistake. In the end, the rooms turned out to be quite stunning, but you never knew, did you?

Grace had phoned Miriam earlier and invited Sadie to lunch with herself and Melissa. Miriam had been pleased.

"Thanks so much for inviting Sadie. She'll be thrilled to go to a restaurant like a grown-up."

They set the date for tomorrow.

Nine

Lunch with Kids; Dinner with Adults

Russell dropped Melissa off at Grace's at ten forty-five the following morning, and at eleven Miriam delivered Sadie. Melissa opened the ladies' door and hugged Sadie, who was dressed all in blue.

Sadie said "You look pretty, Melissa." Melissa, who had recently turned five, twirled around and laughed.

"And you look like a princess," Melissa said. She looked up at Grace. "Come on, Granny Grace, let's go." Moments later, the girls skipped down the path to Grace's car, climbed into the back seat, and pulled the safety straps across their chests. They chattered and giggled all the way into Asheville.

When they reached their destination, Melissa followed Sadie's example and walked sedately into the restaurant. As Grace had anticipated, Melissa behaved impeccably. Sadie spread her napkin on her lap; Melissa followed suit. She spilled nothing and ate slowly, handling her utensils carefully as she tried to master Sadie's European use of fork and knife. She did not scramble from her seat and run about the restaurant, and when the food was slow in coming, she neither whined nor fussed.

Afterward, Grace took them to an inexpensive accessories shop at the mall and bought the girls long, gaudy beads, which they loved. Melissa was a pleasure to be with, instead of a source of aggravation and stress. Deciding that Sadie was the best thing that had ever happened to Melissa, Grace hoped that Miriam and her daughter would stay in Covington for a very long time.

The dinner party on Wednesday evening at the ladies' home was pleasant and seemed to ameliorate the strain between Miriam and Amelia.

Roger's favorite home-cooked meal was meatballs with prunes, with rice smothered in thick gravy. He was in top form and shared his trials and errors at growing vegetables.

"I was totally ignorant, but I thought I was so smart, I didn't need any advice. After all, you put a plant in the ground, water it, and it grows. So I planted broccoli in the heat of summer, in July. Naturally the plants shriveled and died, and I dubbed myself Mr. Brown Thumb and was ready to grass over the garden area. Luckily, Lennie is a professor of horticulture over at Clemson University, and he put me wise to the fact that broccoli needs cool weather."

He looked at Hannah. "And last year, I took your suggestion and planted tropical hibiscus in large containers. They thrived on the deck in full sun and bloomed every day from summer until fall, until a freeze got them. I'll have them again this summer."

"My mother and I once traveled to Barbados in the Caribbean," Miriam said. "What I remember most about that trip was the color of the water and the flowers: bougainvillea, hibiscus, oleander. I loved them all. I had no idea you could grow them in this area."

"Only in the summer," Roger said.

Grace said, "Hannah, Amelia, and I traveled by cruise ship to the Caribbean a year or so ago. I imagine the flowers are the same on all the islands. Amelia took the most gorgeous photographs."

Miriam turned to Amelia. "Oh, will you show them to me, please? I would so love it if you would."

Amelia smiled. "I'd be happy to. After dinner, I'll get out my albums."

They sat on the couch in the living room. Two women who had said hardly ten words to one another since their first encounter were now drawn together by common interests. Heads lowered over the albums, they spoke about the islands, the color of the sky and water, the flowers, and the casual, brightly colored clothing of the people. They forgot for a time that there were others in the room, and it warmed Grace's heart to see them. The ice has been broken, she thought.

"I told myself that when I grew up, I'd move to Barbados," Miriam said. "I'd live in perpetual sunshine and grow beautiful plants. But things change, don't they? As we grow older, our dreams fade."

"I wanted to paint, to be an artist, but I married too young, and my life went in a whole other direction," Amelia said.

"You never went back to it?" Miriam asked.

"No. I never picked up a brush again. Thomas's career took precedence in our lives." She stopped and drew away, remembering that the man she spoke of was Miriam's father. *Easy, Amelia. It's not this young woman's fault.* She shut the album. "Let's do this another time, shall we?"

"I understand," Miriam said. "Another time, yes. Thank you for sharing your gorgeous photographs with me."

One day we will speak of Thomas, Amelia thought. *Miriam must have a hundred questions about her father, and I have questions about her mother. Did she work or did Thomas support them? Was she an educated woman? Yes, one day we will talk—but not yet.*

Ten

THE DEPOT IN MARSHALL

Acting on his mother's suggestion, Roger invited Amelia and Mike to join Grace, Bob, and himself for an evening out at the Depot in Marshall.

"That's something I've been wanting to do for ages," Amelia said. It wasn't until she had called Mike, who agreed to go, that Roger confessed that Miriam would be his date for the evening.

Amelia frowned. "You deliberately tricked me."

Roger bent and kissed her cheek. "Don't be angry with me, please. You're a kind and gracious lady, Amelia, and I love you. I know how hard this whole business with Miriam is for you.

"I've gotten to know her, and I think you'd like her. She's very well educated and well versed in art and music. She loves the theater. Why, she's more like you than either Grace or Hannah are, and little Sadie is just precious." He held her hands in his and looked into Amelia's eyes. "Thank you for agreeing to come with us. It'll be fun, and with all the music and everything going on, you won't have to make conversation with her or with anyone." He squeezed her hands gently.

Amelia smiled up at him. "I'll come, Roger. It's really all right that she will be there. I enjoyed talking with her about the islands. What does one wear to this Depot place, anyway?"

"It's informal. Jeans, I would guess, or comfortable slacks and a shirt."

Before leaving for the Depot, Roger prepared steaks on the new grill he had given the ladies, and which he and Mike had set up on the patio outside the kitchen. Grace and Mike decorated the redwood picnic table with red and white checkered place mats and napkins, and placed tall white tapers and small bowls of red carnations the length of the table.

"Blow on that fire," Mike said to Roger. "Those steaks are cooking too slowly."

"Get on over here and be the bellows, if you'd like," Roger replied.

Mike joined Roger, bent, and huffed and puffed into the fire. "I wouldn't make a very effective big bad wolf, would I?"

While Bob lit the tapers, Roger handed Mike the fork to turn the steaks and dashed into the kitchen, returning minutes later with two baskets of fragrant bread, fresh from the oven.

"Sorry this wasn't ready sooner," Roger said. "As my mother used to say . . ." He winked at Grace. "Better late than never." He poured olive oil into dessert plates filled with herbs, and they tore the bread into small pieces and dipped them into the mixture.

"I do enjoy this, and olive oil is good for you, too," Hannah said.

With great fanfare, Roger declared the steaks done, and Mike carried the heaping platter to the table. They all helped themselves to mashed potatos and corn on the cob.

Grace said, "This has been a real treat for me, not to cook tonight. The steaks are excellent, Roger. Thank you getting them and for cooking them."

"It's a pleasure to do anything for you, Mother," Roger said.

Mike turned to Miriam. "So, Miriam. How do you like our little village of Covington?"

"Very much indeed. Everyone has been so kind to us. Except for our cottage in England with my mother, I've never liked anyplace better."

Amelia leaned forward so that she could see Miriam, sitting two places down from her. "Will you start Sadie in school, with so little of the school year left?"

"I don't know what to do. I was thinking it might be best to wait. I should know what I'll be doing, where I'll be living, by the end of the summer."

"I have a special place by a river where I go to photograph. It's a shallow river, a safe place. May I take Sadie with me one day? I'll get her a simple camera and teach her to take photographs—if you'll let her go with me, and if she'd like to. I wouldn't want to force my interest on her."

"Sadie won't know if it's her interest unless she tries it, now, will she?" Miriam asked softly. "I'd be pleased for her to go with you. I'll ask her."

"I could teach her to bake cookies," Grace said, "and I'm sure Hannah would give her small jobs in the garden at Bella's Park, or even here, this summer. Some of the kids from school work with Hannah at the park in the summer. No sense for Sadie to sit around doing nothing from now until school starts up in the fall."

Hannah wiped her mouth. "Certainly. I'd be happy to."

"Thank you, all of you. What a treat that would be for Sadie," Miriam said. "She'll love all that attention. My mother passed away when Sadie was four." Fleetingly, her eyes met Amelia's. Amelia did not flinch or look away.

"Well, now she can have several grandmothers," Grace said.

They lingered in the quiet peace of the evening until Roger reminded them that they were scheduled to meet some people at the Depot. Everyone rose and cleared the table, and by eight-thirty, those who were going to the Depot squeezed into Roger's SUV and off they drove to Marshall.

Except for the lights shining down on THE DEPOT sign, which hung over the narrow sidewalk, and a light over the entranceway to the building, the main street of Marshall lay dark and silent. Music issued from the wooden building, along with the occasional burst of laughter. No one roamed the narrow sidewalks of the town or dallied outside. The cars, pickups, and vans of customers lined both sides of the two-lane road for several blocks and filled an empty lot beside the Depot. Three blocks down the street, Roger located a parking space and squeezed the SUV into it.

Retha Ward, a member of the preservation and renovation committee, greeted them at the door. Born and bred in Madison County, an artist of some renown, the energetic woman of eighty hugged Roger as if he were an old friend.

"Welcome! You just come on in, here. We're so glad to see you all." She waved them inside.

Bob reached for his wallet, but Retha shook her head. "Now, you just put that wallet back in your pocket. There's no admission charge, but if you'd like, you can drop a contribution into that big glass jar on that table over there."

Bob dropped a five-dollar bill in the three-quarter-full jar, and Roger and Mike followed suit.

"Now, this good-lookin' fellow here's Eugene Louis Wild." Retha's hand rested on the arm of the man beside her. Gene leaned forward and shook hands all around.

"Gene's a native, like me," Retha said. "But he lived for years way up there in Michigan. Now he's come home, like so many of our folks do. This country has a pull on your heart. It's hard to stay away permanently. Gene keeps the Depot's kitchen stocked with supplies. You can get the best foot-long hot dogs you'll ever eat right here, and big juicy hamburgers with all the fixings. We make grilled cheese sandwiches, too, and lots more."

"You got here just at the right time," Gene said. "The

choir's up next. Y'all go in; Forrest has been saving seats for you."

It was intermission. People streamed from the hall and lined up at what had been the ticket booth of the old train station. A FOOT-LONG HOT DOGS sign hung overhead. Grace noticed that many of them carried their food and drinks outside, and she drifted away from Bob and followed a woman out onto a sturdy wooden deck that ran parallel to the French Broad River. Soon the deck filled with people eating foot-long hot dogs, hamburgers, sandwiches, chips, and drinks. They leaned against the railing chatting, and some sat on benches facing the river.

Wide and high from many days of rain in Transylvania County to the southwest, the river roared past, whipping whitecaps to a frenzied dance. On the hillside across the river, lights from homes glittered between the branches of trees.

Grace stuck her head inside and beckoned Bob to join her. "It's lovely out here," she said.

It was cool and pleasant, and they stood at the railing and watched the river. A waning crescent moon hung above the near hills, the narrow valley, and the river.

"I'm glad we came. It's beautiful." Grace tucked her arm through Bob's. "I could stay out here all evening."

"I'd like that, too," he said. "But someone named Forrest has been saving us seats. Let's go in. Looks like people are getting ready to go back into the hall, and Roger's waving at us."

There was something lazy about the night, and people,

including Grace and Bob, ambled slowly back inside. They joined Roger and the others and followed them into the main hall. Chairs had been unofficially labeled as "taken" by shawls, purses, and programs set there by occupants expecting to return, or were guarded by friends or family.

A tall man with the air of someone important beckoned to Roger, and they made their way down the aisle where the man indicated a row about a third of the way back from the stage. Roger introduced them to Forrest Jarrett.

Jarrett shook hands with everyone and slapped Roger on the back. "I'm mighty glad that Roger here brought you all down tonight. We've got a special show. Great gospel singers, and then we'll have Everett Boone's Rocky Creek Band. They play mean old-time country music and bluegrass. They start up the program most nights with bluegrass, and when they get to playing it, you'll want to get up and dance even if you never danced a step in your life."

Forrest sat in the row ahead of them and turned his body so he could talk with them. "I was telling Roger the other day how they were gonna raze this building, and how a group of us formed a committee to save it. We each kicked in twenty dollars. Imagine that. Twenty dollars each, and that's how we got started." He nodded his head and winked. "Then of course we set about contacting the right folks, raised funds, and got grants. We insulated the building and put in a new floor. Now the heat and air-conditioning stay where they should, inside the hall. The acoustics are better now, and it's a whole lot more comfortable. We used to have hard wooden schoolroom seats."

He turned his attention to Amelia. "Miss Amelia, this past

Christmas I bought your photography book. You do mighty good work. Roger tells me you're gonna publish a book about a local family who got caught up in that flash flood we had last year. Terrible business, that flood. Problem is, people keep building their places back along creeks and rivers, and pay no mind to the fact that Madison County's got steep hills that funnel rain right on down into the valleys."

"Yes, I took photographs of the Inman family, before and after the flood," Amelia said. "The flood destroyed everything they had. They had no choice but to leave Old Bunkie Creek. I doubt they'll rebuild there. Besides, the kids like going to school and having friends in town. One of the boys plays football and has a girlfriend."

"Well, that's real good for them, then, isn't it? When's that book of yours coming out?"

"It's in stores now. I'll send you a copy."

"Oh, no, ma'am. It's my pleasure to buy it."

"And mine to give it to you as a gift. Roger has your address?"

People streamed back to their seats, hailing friends and family.

Forrest stood. "I better get outta this seat and back to mine. I'll get my address to you. I'd love for you and your friends to come on by and visit with me. Roger knows where I live, a few miles from here." He joined a couple in the front row, and once seated, turned to wave at them.

"What a nice man." Amelia waved back.

"How do you know him, Roger?" Bob asked. "How do you know all these folks?"

Roger leaned around Miriam. "I find the town of Marshall fascinating. It's the county seat, you know, and has only this one street sandwiched between the railroad tracks that run along the French Broad River and an incredibly steep mountain. Forrest and several members of the committee happened to be standing outside the Depot one day when I came by, and I stopped to chat.

"Forrest worked for many years for the Norfolk and Southern Railroad. When he retired, he came home. He spearheaded the acquisition of the Depot, and they'd just finished the bulk of the renovations."

A hush fell over the room as a dozen men and women in maroon choir robes moved down the aisle toward the platform stage, stepped up onto it, and took their positions. They held up their songbooks and began to sing.

Later, Grace told Brenda that she had never heard "Nearer My God to Thee" or "Just as I Am" sung so sweetly.

When the choir finished, applause thundered through the room. As an encore, the choir offered the ever popular and deeply moving "Amazing Grace," which earned more applause. When the choir trooped from the stage down the aisle, they were followed by low whispers of appreciation.

Then the tone in the room changed. Catcalls and whistles accompanied Everett Boone's five-man Rocky Creek Band down to the stage. The men wore jeans and plaid shirts and carried guitars, one of which was a big bass guitar.

Everett, too, had been born and bred in Madison County, and for thirty years had been a mail carrier in Marshall. Now he stepped to the microphone and began a medley of mournful songs from the forties, including "River of Tears" and Eddy Arnold's "Many Tears Ago," and a song made famous by Roy Acuff, "Pins and Needles in My Heart." People in the audience sang along softly, or closed their eyes and swayed to the music, while others hummed the melodies. Then the mood and the energy shifted as the band switched to bluegrass.

Couples hurried forward to claim a spot on the small dance floor and began to clog, shuffling and tapping, bending forward, leaning back, moving to the music. The stage quickly filled until there was hardly room to move.

"That dance reminds of me an Irish jig," Miriam said to Roger.

"The original settlers here were Scottish and Irish, so it's probably a derivation of an Irish Jig. Want to dance?"

"Thank you, but I'd rather watch." She looked at him, puzzled. "You can do an Irish jig, Roger?"

"Yes. My long-time partner, Charles, who passed away a couple of years ago, taught me. He was English, from the Isle of Wight, actually."

"It looks like it's quite an aerobic workout," Amelia said.

"Quite," Miriam replied. "Before Sadie was born, I taught aerobics classes for a while."

"I used to take aerobic classes. It takes stamina I just don't have anymore," Amelia replied.

Bob nudged Grace. "Want to give it a try up there, honey?"

"I most certainly do not."

Bob shrugged. "Too crowded, anyway." But his feet

tapped the beat. "The rhythm does get to you, though."

It was eleven o'clock when they left their seats and walked down the aisle. People they did not know waved good-bye, and several called, "Come on back, y'all."

Grace nodded and waved back, as did the others.

About a block down from the Depot, three young men, beer cans in hand, leaned against a pickup truck. They poked at one another and their laughter carried a tinge of lewdness. Several six-packs of beer sat on the tailgate of the truck. A fourth man swaggered into the street, then back onto the curb, and back into the street again. A cigarette dangled from his lips. In each hand he carried a can of beer, halting his zigzag performance only to drink first from one can, then the other.

"I thought this was a dry county?" Mike asked.

"It is. I'm surprised they'd drink like that out here on the street. They're high as kites," Bob said.

The swaggering man staggered, pitched forward, and almost fell against Amelia. Mike shielded her with his body and drew her father away into the street.

"Hey, y'all, had a good old time tonight?" The man lifted one beer in a salute. "Anyone wanna beer? We got plenty," he slurred.

Bob held tight to Grace's arm and they quickened their pace. "No, thanks," Bob called back.

"Y'all ain't too friendly, are you?" the man yelled. Then he stumbled and fell facedown into the street. The headlights of a car could be seen approaching. Two of his companions rushed forward, grabbed him under his arms, and yanked him from harm's way, depositing him as indifferently as if he were a bag of cement onto the sidewalk. As beer from both his cans emptied onto the sidewalk, his friends returned to the pickup and continued partying.

Slowly, the car drove past. Shortly after, a siren sounded and two police cars, their lights flashing, pulled alongside the pickup.

"Okay, fellows." A policeman walked up to the men and confiscated the six-packs. "Come on, now, Billy Joe, you know better than this. Whatcha doing breaking the law like this? You guys buy this stuff over in Buncombe County? Come on, now. You all park this pickup over there." He handcuffed Billy Joe. "I'm gonna have to book you. Let's go."

"My pa'll have me out quicker than you can spit," Billy Joe said.

But once handcuffed, he looked forlorn and astonished, as if all of this came as a total surprise. He slumped against the pickup and watched the policeman handcuff another of his pals. Two of the policemen lifted the drunk from the sidewalk and half carried, half dragged him toward their car. Moments later, the pickup was tagged for towing, and all of the drinkers sat behind the grill in the police cars. Then the sirens started and they drove away.

With a collective sigh of relief, the couples from Covington climbed into Roger's SUV and headed home. "I wonder how the cops knew those guys were drinking over here?" Grace asked.

"Someone in the car that went by probably called them on a cell phone. A lot of the folks who live here want Madison

County to stay a dry county. That's what Miss Retha Ward told me," Roger replied. "She's worked hard to help keep liquor stores out. She'd feel good about tonight. The cops did a good job."

"Is that the lady who greeted us when we got to the Depot?" Hannah asked.

"Yes. She's in her eighties, and quite a feisty lady," Roger said. "Her husband owned the Gulf station here. It's years since she retired from the bank, but she goes right on keeping as busy as possible. Gets her out of the house, she says."

"What does she do?" Grace asked.

"She works for a company that offers customers new food products at places like Sam's Club and Ingles Market. You know, when you go by a table and someone offers you cheese or a dip of some kind to taste? And of course, she's chairperson of the Depot Committee."

"Being busy is what keeps you happy. Being happy keeps you young," Hannah said.

Roger took a curve too sharply and they toppled sideways against one another.

"Hey, slow down there, Roger," Bob said.

"Sorry. I didn't realize how sharp some of these curves are." Roger slowed the vehicle to a near crawl.

The night was dark, the road narrow and winding.

Amelia leaned forward and clutched the seat in front of her. "Roads like this scare the dickens out of me. Isn't there another way back?"

"I should have taken the river road. One of the guys in there told me this was a shorter route. We'll be up on the highway soon."

A pole light near a barn offered momentary relief from the inky darkness. Ahead, they could see a squiggly yellow caution sign.

"Back home in England," Miriam said, "my mother and I occasionally vacationed in Scotland. We'd drive up into the mountains on roads like this, but never at night. We had a flat tire once. There we were, sitting on the side of this steep, curvy road with the boot open. We hadn't a clue how to change a tire. Lucky for us, a gentleman came along and his chauffeur changed our tire."

Miriam sighed. "Those men back there scared me. Darren's a drunk, and when he drinks he's mean and dangerous."

Amelia leaned toward Miriam and said softly, "I'm so sorry, Miriam."

Later that evening, back home, Grace and Hannah passed one another in the upstairs hall. Hannah asked, "So what do you think? I noticed that Amelia spoke directly to Miriam several times tonight."

"I think she's moving past anger to see the opportunity that lies ahead with those two."

"From your lips to God's ears," Hannah said.

Eleven

Falling in Love with Sadie

May first. Blossoms, as white and thick as snow, mantled the dogwood trees that shaded the rose, peach, and red azalea shrubs in yards along Cove Road. Robins nested in a hanging basket on the ladies' porch, and hummingbirds visited the feeder that Hannah hung on a tree in the yard.

Amelia stood on the top porch step, her hands circling the handle of the broom, and gazed at the sky. It was amazingly blue, marred only by occasional cirrus clouds moving rapidly across the sky. The searing pain in her chest was gone, as was her anger. The nights spent crying and being utterly miserable over Thomas's betrayal were finally over. Sadie's resemblance to Caroline no longer sent her heart tumbling or brought tears to her eyes. The child warmed her heart, and today Amelia was especially happy. This afternoon at three o'clock she would pick up Sadie, and they would drive to Burnsville to the river.

Inside the house, tucked in its box on the foyer table, sat a shiny new Polaroid camera. Not the drugstore point-and-shoot camera she had anticipated buying, but instant photography! If Sadie could see the result of her shot directly after taking the picture, photography might intrigue her.

Amelia leaned the broom against the wall and headed into the house. At the front door, she paused. What if Sadie found photography boring, as Tyler had when she had tried to teach him? *Stop, Amelia. You're investing too much in this child. First you wanted nothing to do with them, and now it's all about Sadie and her liking what you like. You're ridiculous, a foolish woman desperate for love.*

"No," she said aloud. "I am not desperate for love. There are many people who love me." But the unconscious thought stupefied her, and she stood before the door. Mike, Hannah, and Grace loved her, but they were friends—not family really. Was that enough? Amelia tossed her head in a "what do I care anyway" manner, turned the knob and stepped inside. The phone was ringing.

Mike said, "Amelia. Can you come over to the studio? I'd like you to look at my new photographs, I've just printed them."

"You have new photos?"

"Yes."

"Of what?"

"Come on over and see."

"Sure," Amelia said. "Give me a half hour, okay?"

"That's fine. Thanks a lot. I appreciate it."

He didn't have to thank her. How many times had Mike done kind things, gone out of his way for her? More than she could remember. Amelia hastened upstairs, slipped into slacks and a cotton blouse, and put on a mauve scarf to conceal the scars on her neck caused by the car accident and fire that had killed Thomas. What was wrong with her hair? It just wouldn't stay brushed back. She tucked it behind her ears. How long since she'd had a haircut? She couldn't remember. It was time to have a manicure and facial, a haircut and a pedicure. *I've been so busy hating Miriam. I forgot to take care of myself.*

Amelia ran downstairs and out to the car, then stood there, holding open the door, a blank expression on her face. She'd forgotten her purse and keys. She returned to the house, where the purse and keys lay on the kitchen counter. "I just hate this forgetting things," she muttered.

When she parked on Main Street in Weaverville, across from Mike's Photo Studio, a woman and child were leaving his studio. They stood on the sidewalk, both heads turning left and right before stepping into the street. The woman looked too old to be the child's mother, her grandmother most likely. Perhaps they had made an appointment with Mike for a portrait, or had just had one taken. What a good idea! She'd talk to Mike about a portrait of Sadie, maybe one of herself and Sadie. *There I go again.*

Magnificent black-and-white winter scenes, carefully laid out in two rows on a table, exploded from the paper on which they were printed. They captured the eye and imagination: an animal's footprints sunk deep in a snowdrift; dark twigs sprouting from the snow and casting long shadows; a sunrise seen through a dew-crusted spiderweb; a long-abandoned mill wheel with snow mounded along the upper rim. Next to this lay a photo of bare vines twisted in a vise-like grip around the spokes of the mill wheel, and there were more. Amelia looked down at them in silent appreciation.

"Something wrong? You don't like them?" Mike circled the table. He looked intently at Amelia. "Is the light too harsh?" He picked up a print of a dog, its rear legs half buried in snow, its front paws clawing at a ragged tree trunk as it barked at some unseen creature. "Should I tone down the contrast?"

"Good gracious, no. They're all magnificent! Don't change a thing." Amelia grabbed his arm. "Let me set up a show for you, Mike, please."

"You know I hate being on exhibit. I feel like a clown, standing there shaking hands and smiling at people who haven't a clue what a good photograph is."

"My experience has been that people who come to these shows do so because they have an interest in photography. Some are collectors who buy, but many more come because they appreciate the art itself," Amelia said. "They can be quite subdued, almost reverential events. Please let me set up a show of this work, Mike."

"You'll nag me to death if I don't, won't you?"

She smiled. "I surely will. Your photos are too beautiful to go unnoticed. *You* should be exhibiting in New York, not me. You ought to be writing a column for *Outdoor Photography Magazine*. You deserve top dollar for shots like these." She leaned over the photographs spread out on the table.

Mike clasped both Amelia's hands in his and smiled at her.

"Dear Amelia, I have no interest in the kind of recognition you're talking about. I'm an introvert, remember? I don't like being among a lot of people, especially people I don't know or care about. I make enough money to satisfy my needs. People who come into the shop often buy my work."

"For a pittance of what they're worth," she said.

"I live comfortably enough, and I'm happy with my life."

Amelia dropped onto the old gray sofa that had been in his office forever. "I know that. But I want everyone to see and enjoy your work, to appreciate how talented you are."

"Well, it doesn't bother me one bit if no one knows who I am." Mike sat beside her. "Let's not argue about this. So how's it going with you, and Miriam and the kid? I heard you asking if you could take Sadie to the river with you. Have you two gone yet?"

"We're going today. I decided on a simple Polaroid for her, so she has instant feedback. I thought it might help capture her interest."

"Well, good luck." Mike rose and offered his hand to pull her to her feet. "Out of here, now. I've got to get back to work."

If he doesn't want a show, why did he want me to see his work? I could see it any time, any day. No, I'm not going to drop this. I'm going to arrange a show for Mike.

An excited Sadie climbed into Amelia's car, and they headed toward Burnsville. Questions poured from Sadie. "Is the river we're going to deep?"

"No, not very. You can see the bottom clearly."

"What's on the bottom?"

"Mainly rocks," Amelia replied. "I've also seen some fish."

"Can I take off my shoes and wade in it?"

"No. There are dangerous snakes in the river. Water moccasins, they're called. Once I saw a snake climb up on a rock to sun itself."

"He just climbed up and lay in the sunshine?"

"That's exactly what he did."

"Will he be sunning himself today, do you think?" Sadie asked.

"Probably not. I only saw him that one time," Amelia said.

"Look, Miss Amelia. Look at all that stuff piled up in that yard. What is it?" She twisted around in the seat trying to see the receding mountain of rusting farm tools and heaven knew what else.

"That's a junk yard."

"Can we stop on the way home and look at it?" Sadie asked.

Amelia hesitated, her first impulse an adamant no. Reconsidering, she said, "Maybe we can. If it's not too late."

Sadie clapped her hands. "That would be such fun." Then she suggested that they sing. "I want to sing a song my mama taught me, that her mama used to sing to her."

Amelia smiled. "And what song is that?"

Sadie swayed as she sang. "This is the way the farmer sows his seeds." She mimed sowing. "This is the way he takes his ease." She placed her hands on her hips. "Stamps his foot and claps his hands and turns around to view the land."

"What a nice song," Amelia said.

"Yes, I like it. Do you know any Christmas songs?"

Sadie knew all the words to "Frosty the Snow Man," "Jingle Bells," and "Jolly Old St. Nicholas." Amelia knew all of "Jingle Bells" and a few lines each of the others, but she hummed along as Sadie sang in a sweet, clear voice.

When they stopped, Sadie said, "I love to sing."

Amelia found the little girl enchanting. *Watch yourself, Don't go falling in love with this child. Be careful.*

Amelia parked just off the road. She carried her camera equipment, and Sadie followed her down the slope hauling a cloth bag containing a blanket. They spread it in the shade of a tree, and unpacked packets of fruits, nuts, and several bottles of water. When they settled on the blanket, Amelia presented Sadie with her camera.

The child set the camera on the blanket. "May I go to the river?" she asked.

"Yes, but not too close to the bank."

Sadie ran along the bank of the river, singing some unidentifiable song at the top of her lungs. Finally, winded and breathing hard, she joined Amelia and collapsed at her feet. Amelia handed her a bottle of water.

"Let's settle down, now," Amelia said. "I'll show you how to use your camera."

The little girl simply sat there, the camera in her lap, and looked out at the river, up at the sky. "It's so pretty here," she said.

"Yes, it is." Amelia settled back on her elbows. "And quiet. I like to sit for a while before I take pictures. You see more when you wait and let the river talk to you."

Sadie nodded and leaned on her elbows. They sat for a

time, neither one speaking, and Amelia remembered being young and able to go from running and dancing to thoughtful and quiet. Suddenly she didn't want to photograph the river; she wanted to photograph Sadie.

Down the river a dog appeared on the far bank, dipped its head and drank, looked in their direction, and crossed the river. Next to her, Amelia felt Sadie stiffen.

"That's a chocolate Lab," Amelia said. "They're gentle dogs. If he wanders over our way, I'm sure he won't bother us."

"Are you sure he won't hurt us?" Sadie asked.

Amelia laughed lightly. "Pretty sure. Look he's wagging his tail, and I doubt his owners would let him wander about like this if he were not gentle."

Slowly, stopping to investigate whatever it is that dogs investigate, the animal ambled toward them. Sadie snuggled close until her small body pressed against Amelia's. Amelia slipped her arm about her. "Don't be afraid," she said.

"I am, just a little," the child replied.

The dog reached their blanket, its tail wagging. It was a female and, as Amelia had hoped, quite gentle. Moments later, she flopped onto the blanket near their feet.

Amelia leaned forward and patted her head. "What's your name, pretty girl?" she asked.

"Silly." Sadie giggled. "She can't talk." She bent forward and cautiously touched the smooth hair on the dog's back. The tail wagged harder, and the dog turned its eyes on the child. "She's got gold-colored eyes."

Clouds moved lazily across the sky; the river slowly slid

past. The dog lay between them, its head in Sadie's lap.

Well, Amelia thought, we won't shoot pictures today. She felt a momentary pressure. This was not the way she'd planned it, but what difference did it make? There would be other places where they could shoot. The day was good just the way it was. Sadie had been afraid of the dog, but now loved petting it and was having a wonderful afternoon. That's all that mattered.

Rising, Amelia brushed off her slacks and picked up her camera. She shot a roll of Sadie and the dog.

Sadie slept on the trip home, the camera in her lap, the trash yard forgotten. She never stirred until they pulled into Max's driveway, where Miriam waited. She ran to open the door.

"Mama." The child yawned. "I had the best time in my whole life." She lifted her arms to be carried, and Amelia grabbed the camera lest it tumble to the ground.

"I'll call you," she whispered to Miriam.

A half hour later, lying in a hot tub, Amelia said, "I had the best time in a long time, too." She closed her eyes and let the water wrap about her.

Twelve

Here's My Address

As an only child, Roger had prayed for a sister. From their first meeting, he felt a connection to Miriam that moved them rapidly beyond strangers to friends. Now, as they ambled through the Grove Arcade, a magnificently restored building in the heart of Asheville, Roger stopped occasionally to direct Miriam's attention to a handturned wooden bowl, a blown-glass vase, a handmade quilt in another store window. Shops in the arcade featured local arts and crafts, as well as groceries and restaurants. Offices occupied the second floor, and luxury apartments crowned the multistory building.

"I can't tell you how very much I appreciate all the time you've spent with Sadie and me," Miriam said. "But I wouldn't want your mother to resent me for consuming your time. Grace is a wonderful woman, and she's been very kind to us."

"My mother doesn't anger easily, and she isn't one to hold

resentments," Roger replied. "We're going out for dinner tonight, just she and I. She'll ask me a hundred questions about my life in South Carolina and be happy."

They stood at the window of an artwork and crafts shop. "That's a gorgeous throw, isn't it?" He leaned close to the window. "The colors are wonderful, like a rainbow. Let's go in. I'd like to get that for my mother."

Inside, Miriam ran her hand along the fabric. "It's lovely and so soft," she said.

The saleswoman came over. "Hi, may I help you?"

"Yes, I'd like this wrapped as a gift." Roger handed her the throw and followed her to the counter.

Miriam drifted about the shop, admiring metal sculpture, wooden bowls and bookends, woven tapestries. She stopped to look at photographs: layered mountains shrouded in mist, rhododendrons in full bloom spilling down a hillside, hardwood trees in full fall color. On a table below lay several books by Celia H. Miles. Miriam picked up *Mattie's Girl: An Appalachian Childhood* and another of the author's books, *Sarranda*, a story about the struggle for survival of a woman left behind in the mountains of Appalachia during the Civil War.

Roger came to stand beside her, package in hand.

"I'm going to get these books," Miriam said. "I'd like to get more of a feel for this area and what it must have been like growing up here."

Miriam opened the first book. "It says here that this little girl's brother and his pals were known as 'rapscallions.' That's a word I'm not familiar with."

"Probably means they were mischievous," Roger said.

They found a restaurant at the far end of the arcade and shared a wickedly rich dessert. "I'd really love to make this area my home," Miriam said. "Maybe I could get a job teaching elementary school. I used to teach, but that was years ago, before Sadie was born. I'm probably too rusty, and I'm not licensed in this state."

"I could take you to the department of education, and you could ask. Maybe they'd hire you as a substitute teacher. That would allow you to hone your skills and build your confidence. I'm sure you were a wonderful teacher," Roger said.

"You're so kind, Roger. But I'll wait to see what happens. Who can tell if I'll even be able to stay? God bless Max and Hannah, but my funds are running low. I haven't the means to take a lease on an apartment or a small house. Before I do anything, I need to feel some sense of certainty that Darren isn't going to come after us. I can't lie to an employer and say I'm here to stay, when I might have to leave in a big hurry."

"Miriam." Roger slipped a card into her hand. "I've been meaning to give you this. Salem, where I live, is way off the beaten path. You'd be safe there. If you ever have any cause to be afraid, just come. I've printed directions on the card with my home and cell phone numbers. It's an hour and a half from here by car. You don't have to call, just come. I keep a house key under the metal urn on the front porch. You can let yourself in anytime."

Her chin quivered and tears flooded her eyes. "How can I ever thank you? Oh, thank you so much." She leaned over and kissed his cheek. *Why*, she wondered, *are so many of the really kind and good men gay?*

The evening was balmy and pleasant. Roger escorted Grace into the Weaverville Milling Company Restaurant and took a table outside on the patio, where Grace ordered plum chicken and Roger decided on steak.

"Things are good for me," Roger told her. "Each semester, I enroll in one or two horticulture classes at Clemson University. In time, I may have a whole new career. Imagine going from being an engineer to being a horticulturist." He laughed. "I wonder what Charles would think about all this?"

"Charles would be pleased that you are happy."

"I think so, too. The interesting thing is, I hadn't a clue I had an interest in plants until I bought my land. Funny, the twists and turns life takes."

"Do you see much of that Clemson professor we met at your house?" Grace asked.

"Lennie? Sometimes I take a class from him. Sometimes if he's on campus and I have a class, we'll have lunch at the university cafeteria. But he's busy and he lives in Pendleton, the other side of Clemson."

"How long a drive is it from Salem to Clemson?" Grace asked.

"About forty-five minutes. I take the back road along Lake Keowee, which is always a pleasant drive. You ought to see how the area is built up. On both sides of the road, wherever there's a finger of water, there are huge homes being built.

With all that housing, I might decide to operate a small, highly personalized landscaping business. I'd do the design, subcontract the actual physical landscaping work and the plants, but I'd supervise it all."

"I love the sound of that." Grace unfolded her napkin and spread it on her lap, then stirred her iced tea. "I'm happy you're happy. Life's too short to work at something you don't like."

"How do you know? You've never worked, at least not when I was a kid."

"Your father didn't always like his work. He stayed with one company all of his working life, but his bosses changed. Some were good men, fair and decent, and some were stinkers who made life miserable for your father—especially as he got older and the bosses got younger. He'd complain, and I'd get all upset, especially when he'd come home depressed and with a splitting headache. I used to urge him to quit.

"He'd say, 'They come and go, Gracie. This one'll be gone before long, just you wait and see.'

"And he was right. That young boss would find greener pastures and things would settle down for a while. But I guess I never stopped worrying about when the next lousy boss would arrive."

Reaching over, Roger patted her hand. "You were always a worrywart, Mother."

"That's what your father used to say. But we are who we are. You were always finicky about things, like how your socks were rolled and where they sat in your sock drawer. You remember that time I dumped them in the drawer? I was rushing to go somewhere, but you accused me of doing it deliberately because, you said, I was angry with you. About what, I can't recall. Can you?"

He laughed. "What a memory you have. I remember the incident and being upset, but not the rest. However did you put up with me? I was such a prig."

She looked into his eyes. "I loved you. I loved you with my whole heart and soul, and I still do, Roger." Her voice cracked.

"And I love you, Mother."

The waiter arrived with their dinners and the conversation lightened. Roger spoke about going into Greenville to the Center for the Performing Arts, and seeing *Doubt*, a controversial drama about whether a priest was gay or not. It was the touring company straight from Broadway. And he also had tickets for an upcoming musical, *A Light in the Piazza*.

"I thought I'd be culturally deprived, moving to the country. But it's amazing how fast they get touring companies going," he said. "There's no need to run up to New York to go to the theater."

"Do you drive all the way to the theater alone?" Grace asked.

"Sometimes Lennie goes, and sometimes I go with other friends—a couple who live just down the road from me."

While they waited for dessert, Grace said, "I think Amelia's gone quite mad for Sadie. She took Sadie to the river, and all she shot was Sadie and a dog who happened by." Grace leaned forward and lowered her voice as if what she was about to relate was some closely held secret. "I think Amelia is thinking about asking them to live with us. Hannah suggested that we add another room off our guest room. Bob thinks we ought to build a cottage like his, but a bit larger, so they could be independent and yet close to us. What do you think?"

"I like the idea of the cottage. You ladies have a routine, and you don't get in one another's way. A child underfoot might be tedious after a while. The cottage is a great idea, and if they ever move out, you have a rental. Either way, though, it would be a boon for Miriam. I doubt that she has much money."

"Brenda is going to offer Miriam a job as a substitute teacher in the fall. That way she can get around the licensing business. Miriam was certified to teach K through 5 in Connecticut. And yes, indeed, the cottage would be a good investment for us, if she meets someone later on and gets married."

"Sounds like you ladies have it all figured out," he said, with a twinkle in his eye. But were they ignoring the fact that Darren hung in the wings of Miriam's life, threatening to disrupt whatever plans she might make, whatever dreams she might have? He had come to love her as a sister. She would always be welcome in his home, and he would protect and shelter them both as best he could.

Thirteen

MIRIAM REFLECTS

Miriam stared up at the ceiling, remembering the day a doctor called to tell her that her mother had entered a London hospital for exploratory surgery, and that she would like Miriam to come as soon as possible.

Startled and upset, she hadn't asked what exploratory surgery meant. Instead she'd cried, then picked up the phone and made plane reservations for herself and four-year-old Sadie. Why had Stella not said one word about being sick? They had been so close, and she had hoped her mother would come to live in America. But then when the abuse started, rather than be honest with her mother, she had hidden the truth.

Well, the doctors would find whatever was wrong, and make her well. Sadie couldn't lose her grandmother; they hardly knew one another. She had taken Sadie to London only once before, when Sadie was two. Her mother had adored Sadie, sung to her and played with her. It had been a joyful time for them all. Stella had looked wonderful, youthful and vital. How could she now be sick and hospitalized?

Miriam could see the small cottage in the suburbs of London in which she had lived with her mother. Stella had raised her daughter to believe that her father's parents had been older when he was born, and had passed away at about the time that their son entered the navy. They had been very proud of their Thomas, she said. Unfortunately, all of their family photos had been lost in a fire, the shock of which, Stella was certain, had led to their deaths.

A lavender-blooming vine covered the entranceway to her mother's lovely garden, and a white picket fence ran along the road. Stella's garden was beautiful and drew the attention of passersby. Stella credited the garden to Miriam's paternal grandmother—her make-believe grandmother, as she would discover.

"She was a born gardener, your Gran Rosalie," Stella had said. "Isn't it wonderful that you've inherited her green thumb? Look how your bean has taken root and grown." Miriam went on to plant marigolds and had been thrilled by the speed at which they grew and by their crowns of thick golden blossoms.

Stella had said to Mrs. Treadwell, their neighbor and close friend, "Wouldn't you know, the child has her grandmother's green thumb."

Later, when Miriam knew the truth and had come to terms with it, she admired the way her mother had created a fantasy family, giving her deep roots and traditions. The vivid stories brought grandparents to life for Miriam and had harmed no one.

Sadie turned in the bed beside her, bringing her back to reality. As the child settled into a deep sleep, Miriam returned to memories of the day that she had received the news of Stella's illness.

"Put that confounded phone down," Darren had shouted.

Even these many years later, remembering his voice, his tone, his menacing manner, sent Miriam's heart skittering. But she had defied him, even when he towered over her, breathing hard, his eyes bright with anger.

"Do as I tell you, this minute. Put down that phone. You're not going anywhere." Darren tore the receiver from her hand and slammed it down. It had fallen and dangled above the floor by its short cord.

Her concern and love for her mother bolstered her courage. For the first and only time, she dared to stand up to him. "Don't you tell me what to do. This is my mother, and I will go to her now, and I will take Sadie."

Surprisingly, he weaseled out, apologized, and she kept those reservations. She had been proud of herself. It had been the beginning of the end of her life with Darren.

Miriam's heart broke when she saw her mother. A formerly robust woman, Stella lay there, her arms thin as sticks, her color wan, her lips a thin, chapped line. Miriam rested her head on the side of the hospital bed and wept.

The medical team asked her to step into the hallway, where they shook their heads and expressed regrets. "She came to us too late. Cancer has consumed every organ in your mother's body. We're sending her home. It's a matter of weeks, maybe two months. You'll need Hospice. They'll keep her comfortable."

Once Stella was settled at home, the two women talked. "I can sense from your letters, the things not said, that there's trouble in your household," Stella said.

Miriam nodded and the tears came.

Bright spots of pink appeared on her mother's cheeks. "Tell me the truth, all of it," Stella demanded, and Miriam poured out her heart.

"Don't go back to him, to America, Miriam. Don't raise Sadie in an abusive home." The effort she expended left Stella limp, but her mother's eyes blazed. "You and Sadie must not go back to him."

That night, alone in the silence of her childhood bedroom, Miriam struggled with the decision. Yet she could not decide, not with her mother so ill. She watched, helpless and frightened, as Hospice administered ever-stronger medication to quell Stella's pain.

There were fewer lucid moments as the days passed, and it was during one of those times of clarity that Stella gripped her hand and confessed the truth about her father.

Shock stripped Miriam of speech. Then came the anger and a deep sense of having been betrayed. Her entire life had been a lie! She fled her mother's room and paced the house. When she grew calm enough to speak to Stella, she found it impossible not to accuse her.

"You lied to me, all those years. How could you do this to me? You lied to me." She regretted her words, her tone of voice, her anger. How many times had she wished she could retract them?

From eyes sunken deep in a gaunt face, tears streamed down her mother's hollow cheeks. "Yes, my darling," she whispered. "I lied to you. I wanted to give you roots and security. Please, please, forgive me." She closed her eyes then, and drifted away, the medication wafting her to peaceful, pain-free sleep.

Little time was left to them, and reason prevailed. Whatever her mother had done, she had acted to protect and shield her daughter. Better a dead naval officer than no father; better the name Declose on her birth certificate than her mother's maiden name. Better a make-believe family from whom she had inherited many positive traits, than no sense of history or belonging. Through her grief, disbelief, and shock, Miriam had begun to understand.

Over the following weeks, in fifteen minutes here, thirty minutes there, like a serialized, eagerly anticipated movie, Stella filled in the pieces. She had been secretary to an executive in London with whom Thomas Declose did business.

"From the instant I saw him, I loved him," she said, and a look of peace briefly filled her eyes. "I can't explain such a thing, but the draw was so powerful that all of my values, everything I had been taught, everything I believed to be right, vanished. I did not care that he was married. I would have been his mistress forever. But then I became pregnant. We hadn't planned on that, and it brought our relationship to an end. I wanted more than he could give me."

She explained that Thomas had been honest from the beginning, had said that their relationship could never be more than an affair. "He was married to a wonderful woman, a good woman, and they had lost a child. That loss had nearly killed his wife Amelia, and he would never leave her. He suggested that I have an abortion, but I refused."

It was then that she gave Miriam his address and extracted the same promise that she had made to Thomas. "Contact your father only if you find yourself in the most dire of circumstances. If Darren ever strikes you again, you must find your father. Promise me!"

After the funeral, Miriam and Sadie had returned to America. She continued to live with Darren and had not heeded her mother's pleas, had not tried to locate her father.

"Thomas and Amelia will help you. She's a good woman. She will understand. Enough time has passed, and you are not to blame for the sins of your parents," Stella had said.

Why, then, had she failed to contact Thomas and Amelia after Darren struck her so hard across the face that she pitched backward, smashed her head against the wall, and slid, nearly unconscious, to the floor? Was it because he had kneeled beside her, cradled her in his arms, cried, apologized, and assured her that he loved her; and like so many battered wives, who fall prey to the devious techniques abusers use, wanted and even needed to believe him?

In a flash, Miriam understood why she had not contacted her father early on. Fear of rejection had stayed her hand from picking up that phone. Possibility offered hope; rejection was final. If Thomas had refused to talk to her, if Amelia refused to help her, there would be no place to turn. She would be irrevocably alone.

What a fool she had been. Had her father been alive she might have had the family she longed for, instead of years of abuse and a life on the run.

Well, regret was useless, especially as the tide seemed to be turning. Amelia had changed. She looked at her now, not away from her or through her, as she had done. She spoke kindly to her, and clearly she cared for Sadie. Perhaps in time Amelia would come to care for her, too.

Miriam looked at her child and her heart filled with love. They would make it somehow, and someday, please, God, they would be free of Darren Smith. Then she would at last be able to make a productive life for herself, a life where she could laugh and sing and be happy.

Fourteen

Long Ago and Far Away

The velvet-red Chrysler Imperial roses Hannah had planted along the driveway filled the air with fragrance. Folks walking past the house stopped and bent to smell their sweetness. A young woman who was married in Cove Road Church carried Hannah's roses down the aisle, and a girl of perhaps seventeen stopped after church one Sunday to ask if she might have a rose or two for her mother, who was ill in the hospital. Hannah sent her off with a dozen.

Each morning, Sadie hastened across the road to the ladies' porch, where Amelia waited to pin a rosebud on her shirt. Each day, they sniffed it and chatted earnestly about whether this rose was as fragrant as yesterday's. Amelia ached to say to the child, "Please don't call me Miss Amelia. Call me Granny or Grandma." Perhaps one day she'll spontaneously call me Granny, Amelia thought, resisting the urge to scoop Sadie into her arms.

One day Miriam called and invited Amelia out for lunch.

When Amelia accepted, Miriam said, "I will pick you up at eleven o'clock tomorrow."

"Where are we going?"

"It's a surprise," Miriam said.

The next day, they drove into Asheville and crossed the bridge to the western section of the city, where, after several turns, they followed a narrow one-lane road to a cottage tucked behind an evergreen hedge. Above the arbor entrance, the sign read LONG AGO AND FAR AWAY.

"What a charming place," Amelia said. "I had no idea it existed. However did you find it?"

"Roger brought me here. I especially like it because it's a cottage restaurant, and it reminds me of home."

Amelia stood for a moment and studied the sign. "Long ago and far away. I remember a song with those lines." She hummed a few measures, than sang:

Long ago and far away.
I dreamed a dream one day.

She closed her eyes and began to sway as she sang, her scarf billowing out behind her. She paused, opened her eyes, and looked into Miriam's surprised face. "The last line of that refrain is, 'You're here at last.'" Yes, she thought, you *are* here at last. You and Sadie are my heart's desire. "There are other verses, but I don't remember them."

They stepped through the arbor and followed a winding brick path to the front door. "Roger said that your friend Mike brought him here when he first came to Asheville. On Saturday nights there's a man who looks to be a hundred years old, who sings medieval English ballads: 'Barbara Al's Cruelty,' 'The Bailiff's Daughter of Islington,' 'Lord Randall,' 'The Wife of Usher's Well' are but a few of them." She began to sing softy.

There lived a wife at Usher's Well
And a wealthy wife was she:
She had three stout and stalwart sons,
And sent them o're the sea.

They hadn't been a week from her,
A week but barely ane.
When word came to the earline wife
That her three sons were gane.

"They died?" Amelia asked. "All of them died? How terrible for the poor woman."

Miriam nodded. "It's a long tale, and sad. They're all sad, these old ballads." She changed the subject. "I do miss Roger. He was like a brother to me. I always wished I had a brother or a sister."

"I, too, was an only child, and I longed for a sibling and prayed for one," Amelia said. "We didn't have much choice in that matter, though, did we?"

Why does every innocent remark take me back to Thomas and the whole sordid business? I must stay focused on the fact that Miriam had nothing to do with any of it.

Miriam laughed. "We certainly did not."

The interior of the restaurant mirrored the charming exterior: chintz curtains on mullioned windows, floral-covered armchairs set about round tables, and soft lighting.

The waiter seated them near a window, in the center of which glowed a coat of arms.

Amelia squinted at the menu. "I should have brought my reading glasses. I think I'd like a salad. Can I trouble you to read this for me?" She handed her menu to Miriam, who read down the list of salads and dressings.

They ordered chicken salads, and the waiter filled Miriam's glass with sweet iced tea. Amelia ordered a pot of hot tea, which came complete with tea leaves and a strainer.

Amelia spread her napkin across her knees and settled back in the armchair. "This is quite comfy. I bet people are in no hurry to leave. Well, now tell me, how do you like Covington?"

"It's rather a hamlet compared to Hartford, Connecticut, where we lived, but it's exactly what I needed. I like it very much," Miriam replied.

"How long do you think you might stay?" Amelia's tone was casual, but she waited anxiously for Miriam's reply.

Miriam leaned forward, elbows on the table, her chin resting on coupled hands. "If it were up to me, I'd stay forever."

"Tell me about your life growing up. You have no siblings—did your mother ever marry, I mean later on?" Amelia flushed, but Miriam seemed unfazed by the question.

"No, I am sorry to say she did not. I cannot recall her ever dating anyone. It's rather a shame, isn't it? She was a very attractive woman."

"I could see that from her picture. What did she do? I mean, did she work?" *Had Thomas supported them?*

"She worked for an executive at an oil company in

London, and rode the tube into the city every day. When I was little a neighbor, Mrs. Treadwell, looked after me. When I started school, she drove me there in one of those motorcycles with a sidecar. We wore goggles and helmets and fancy scarves that blew in the wind behind us. That was fun, and all the kids at school envied me. Mrs. Treadwell was like an aunt to me, or even a gran. She baked incredible cookies and cherry pies, and brought them for tea on Saturdays.

"We lived in a vine-covered cottage outside the city. Now and then I see a film on the telly, one of those black-and-white forties films, with a cottage that so resembles ours that I wonder if it is, and I wonder who lives there now."

Amelia swallowed hard. "Is that where your mother met Thomas, through her work? Thomas used to travel often to London on fund-raising junkets for the Red Cross."

Miriam's cheeks flushed. She sipped her iced tea, then set the glass down. Her eyes met Amelia's. "From what little my mother told me, she met him at work."

"Oh."

Miriam leaned forward. "Are you sure you want to talk about these things, Amelia?"

Amelia's brow furrowed. "How else will I put this behind me? Unresolved issues, unanswered questions, haunt us. How can you and I have a relationship if every time I am with you, I'm wondering about this or that? We should be able to talk about this like civilized people. It happened a long time ago."

Miriam sighed. "When my mother first told me the truth, I didn't believe her. I thought she was delirious, the result of medications. When I finally accepted that she was rational, I was incredibly angry. How could she have lied to me all those years? I was awash in anger, confusion, disbelief, denial, a deep sense of having been betrayed. That was probably the strongest feeling—betrayal—and it hung on for a long time." Miriam fell silent.

Amelia waited.

"But mother was dying of cancer. How could I tell her how I felt, or the depth of my anger and disappointment?"

"Cancer? Oh, my dear, I am so sorry. Of course you couldn't express your honest feelings at a time like that. How hard it must have been for both of you."

"I went back to England to be with her. I had no idea she was so ill; she never told me. She put off seeing a doctor until it was too late. The surgeon who operated on her told me that there was nothing he could do. When he recommended Hospice, I knew she hadn't long to live. All I wanted was to be with her, to do anything I could to help make her comfortable."

"I'm sure it meant everything to her to have you with her, to talk with you," Amelia said.

"So she could make her deathbed confession?" Miriam was surprised at her bitterness. After all these years, was she still angry with her mother?

"Perhaps she always intended to tell you, but illness caught up with her before she could do so," Amelia said.

"Anger's a funny thing. I raged at her dying and leaving me; I needed her. And I raged because she had lied to me, because my whole life had been a lie. It took a long time to even begin to forgive her. Odd, isn't it, that I never blamed him?"

Just as I didn't blame Thomas, but vented my rage on Miriam and Sadie. Are we so schooled in putting men on pedestals, giving them the benefit of the doubt, that we do so way beyond the time they deserve it?

Miriam continued, "When I arrived in England, I told my mother about my life with Darren, and she wanted me to leave him on the spot. Several days later, she asked me to sit beside her. She instructed me not to interrupt her, no matter what I might feel or want to say, until she had finished relating a matter of great importance.

"Then she told me about my father. I often think that she would have taken her secret to her grave, had I not told her about Darren. That's when she gave me the only phone number and address that she had for you, and insisted that I promise never to search for my father, except under the most dire of circumstances. I was *living* in dire circumstances, and still I stalled and stalled, and waited too long."

"Yes, my dear," Amelia said softly. "Thomas died before Sadie was born, but he would have adored her." *He would have been so happy to have a daughter, too, and he would have adored her, as well.* Amelia sat upright, her back pressed against the back of the chair. "We could have helped you, been there for you. Oh, I'm sure I would have yelled and carried on at first, but then I'd have gotten past it, and we could have been a family. But that's behind us now. I hope you and I will be good friends."

"I'd like that," Miriam said. "I'd like that very much."

As the waiter set their salads before them, Miriam continued, "After my mother died, I hoped that with the sale of her cottage, I could leave Darren. But the cottage was mortgaged to the hilt, and after the debts were paid, there wasn't enough for me to start a new life. All I had was family jewelry from her mother, which I hid from Darren. I sold it when I knew that I had to run as far from him as possible."

"And you're here now, my dear, and you're divorced from that bastard. Brenda Tate is the principal of our elementary school, and she's a good friend of ours. I'm sure if you decide to remain in Covington, she would hire you to teach."

Miriam's voice trembled. "If I knew he wouldn't track me here, I'd stay. I would never leave." Reaching across the table, she grasped Amelia's hand. "You don't know him, Amelia. He's capable of killing us all."

"We will do whatever we can to protect you. Max has spoken to the sheriff and they'll keep an eye out. They can't arrest him without cause, but they can be alert to what he does. No one wants to see you hurt."

"I know that," Miriam said. "But they don't know how devious Darren is, or how he drinks and how violent he can be."

"Well, let's enjoy our lunch and talk about more pleasant things now."

They sat for a long while swapping stories of growing up, of having only one good friend, and of their solitary childhoods. The old house on the cliff above the Atlantic coast of Rhode Island, where Amelia had grown up, came alive as she described its turrets and many rooms, some kept locked and unused. She spoke about her stunning but distant socialite mother, her loving but too often absent father, and the grandmother whom she had adored.

Miriam shared tales of summers with her mother on the

English coast, of vacations on the Isle of Wight, a trek through Wales, and one very special holiday on the Mediterranean coast of Spain, an area familiar to Amelia, who had vacationed there with Thomas. It pleased Miriam to think that she and her father might have dined in the same cafe, attended the same theater, walked the same charming, narrow streets of Barcelona.

Finally, Miriam said, "Would you be comfortable telling me about my father and my real grandparents? What was my father like? Was he tall? Was he witty or formal? Did he like to dance?"

Why wouldn't Miriam want to know about Thomas? He was her father. His parents were her grandparents. "Yes, I can do that," Amelia said. "Just a moment. My throat's a little dry." She poured herself another cup of tea and sipped, then set the teacup down.

"First, his parents—your grandparents. They lived in Vermont, near Manchester, in a town called Ludlow. His mother, Margaret, didn't like the water, especially the Maine coast, which is where Thomas's father, Henry, was born.

"Henry was a professor at a college. She never worked outside the home, though she was active in her church. She was a fine seamstress and made clothes for the church bazaar. They were a devoted couple. Margaret was soft-spoken and always kind to me, but not given to open affection. My father-in-law loved people, loved to talk, and loved teaching. Students would gather at their home on Sunday afternoons for coffee and cake. I had a lot of photos of them. They were quite handsome, both of them.

"Thomas was 'a change-of-life baby,' his mother used to say. I think what I liked most about them was that they weren't driven people. They were satisfied with their lives, their friends, and their community. His mother seemed dull at times, limited, and certainly not adventurous, but as I got to know her, I came to admire, respect, and love her. I admired her grace under pressure and her loyalty to her friends and family. Caroline's death was a bitter blow to them."

"They seem like people I would have loved."

"I think you would have. And they would have treasured you."

"Thank you for telling me about them."

"It was good to speak of them," Amelia said. "I never do, and they deserve to be spoken of and remembered." She leaned forward and rested her hand on Miriam's. "Perhaps one day, when Darren is no longer a threat to you, we could take a trip to Vermont, visit their former home and where they're buried. Would you like that?"

"Would you really do that for me?"

"I'd love doing it with you. It's a visit long overdue." Amelia paused. "Anything else you'd like to know about them?"

"Not right now. Perhaps later, after I think about them for a while, I'll have questions." She leaned forward. "And my father? What was he like?"

"Your Sadie has his blue eyes and the cleft in his chin. He stood six feet three inches in stocking feet. He was distinguished and handsome, and a very smart dresser. And yes, he was witty, a great conversationalist, and a fine dancer. He was a good father when he was at home, and he would read to Caroline at bedtime."

Cast into the past, Amelia could see the vine-covered walls of the small villa in the French countryside where they had spent their summers. The smell of fresh-mown hay wafted back through the years. Huge bunches of wildflowers filled big, round pottery crocks that sat on tables throughout the living and dining rooms. Those had been happy summers, filled with love and promise.

Amelia pulled herself back to the present. "He might be dressed in a tux and a limousine might be waiting for us downstairs, but he'd be upstairs in Caroline's bedroom tucking her in for the night."

"He sounds wonderful," Miriam said. *I don't want her to dwell on Caroline. It will only make her sad and throw a pall over this lovely visit we are having.* "Where did you two meet? How old were you? Was it love at first sight?" Miriam remembered Stella saying that she had fallen in love with Thomas at first sight.

"We met at a ball, a fund-raiser for the arts. I was very young, only eighteen, and he was twenty-nine and already a development director for the local opera society." She sipped her tea again and smiled at Miriam. "It's a gift, you know, being a successful fund-raiser. Wealthy folks are hounded for donations for this or that worthy cause: cancer research, children's hospitals, the arts. Thomas excelled at what he did. He was low-key, attentive, a good listener, and never pushy. He developed a solid relationship with his clients. We always referred to his most trusted donors as his clients." She paused and looked off into the distance for a moment. "You asked about love at first sight. I was flattered, of course. He was older, more sophisticated and mature than I was. But love at first sight?" Amelia shook her head. "No. I can't say that it was like that—not for me, and I don't think it was for Thomas, either. We met again at another social function; my parents were very active in community events. He asked me out for dinner. Our romance grew slowly."

"What did he do for fun?" Miriam asked

"Thomas loved to played tennis. We both did, until I twisted my ankle very badly and tore a ligament. I never went back to the game, but he played until he was in his fifties." *What else did he do for fun? When we vacationed, he stayed in touch with the office. We'd be at dinner, and he'd be called to the telephone.* "He really only had one other interest outside of his work," Amelia said.

"What was that?" Miriam leaned forward, eager for all the information she could garner.

"He was a stamp collector, a philatelist."

"I never knew anyone who collected stamps."

"That was the way he relaxed. Thomas would sit for hours over his stamp collection. There were people all over the world with whom he traded, or from whom he bought stamps. After he died, I kept his stamp collection. But sadly, that was lost when we had that awful fire a few years ago."

They sat quietly for a time. Then Miriam asked, "Was my father a kind man, a generous person?" She hesitated. "Was he a good son, a good husband?"

Amelia nodded. "He was an only child, so the fact that he

left his hometown and hardly ever returned, hardly ever saw his elderly parents once he began to travel, makes me wonder about his being a good son. Yes, he supported them financially in their later years, took care of their medical needs, but emotionally, I would have to say no. He neglected them by being so far away.

"As a husband, he was kind and generous. For the first few days after we lost Caroline, he never left my side. I think he was afraid that I would kill myself." Amelia squared her shoulders and continued.

"We once went to India several weeks after a devastating storm. High winds had wreaked havoc, and there had been flooding. By the time we arrived in New Delhi, people were becoming ill. The rivers were sewers. An epidemic was under way, but no one had told us that.

"Thomas felt we would be safe. We were staying at a very fine hotel, where they brought in bottled water and Western food. Caroline wouldn't be going out into the streets. I hadn't wanted to take her with us. We had argued about this, but he'd been away a lot and didn't want to leave her yet again. When Caroline became ill, her symptoms were not at all like those commonly going around, and the doctors there couldn't make a firm diagnosis. We were heading home to a hospital in England . . ."—Amelia's eyes misted—"when she died in my arms, on the plane." *There, I've said it and I didn't break down.* "Caroline had developed a massive infection from an insect bite, they said. I don't remember much about those days; only the pain of it.

"I went slightly crazy. No, I went totally crazy. I cursed and screamed at Thomas and blamed him. Later, of course, I apologized, but how do you heal the effect of such bitter words? I'd been irrational with grief, and he knew that, but he blamed himself, too, and my diatribe certainly didn't help. He was gentle then, and more thoughtful of me when he was at home. That was when he began to travel more often and for longer periods. That's probably when he met your mother."

Miriam listened carefully, trying to match dates and years. They *had* met straightaway after the death of Amelia and Thomas's little daughter. Maybe it was guilt that drove him into her mother's arms. But wouldn't an affair have compounded his guilt? Still, she now understood why her father had not left Amelia, no matter how much he might have loved her mother.

"My goodness." Amelia shuffled the silverware on the table. "I am sorry. I hadn't intended to go on and on like that."

The restaurant had grown busy and noisy, so they paid the bill. As they walked back to the car, Amelia asked, "Did Sadie ever have a bad experience with dogs? She seemed quite frightened when we were at the river and the dog appeared and started toward us."

"A neighbor's dog once barked loudly and came running at her. He was a large brown dog, but he didn't hurt her. He just scared her."

"This dog was also brown and fairly large." Amelia unlocked the car doors and slid inside. "But by the time we left the river, Sadie and the dog were the best of friends."

Fifteen

The Good Times End

"When days are worrisome and sad, time hangs heavy. When days are happy, time flies," Amelia said, describing to Grace the difference before and after her lunch with Miriam. "It was special. We really communicated. There was so much we each wanted to know—me about her mother, she about her father and his parents."

It pleased Grace that Amelia could now so easily refer to Thomas as Miriam's father. She had come a long way.

As the days passed, as they visited and chatted, Amelia and Miriam discovered their mutual enjoyment of music and art, their love of nature and of Stephen King's new mysteries. They loved the theater and shopping, and Miriam found it impossible to dissuade Amelia from buying yet another pretty dress or doll or new game or book for Sadie.

After the visit to the Depot, the ladies and their men, plus Mike, Miriam, and Sadie, began to share dinners: sometimes at the ladies' home, sometimes at Max's, and some Sundays,

Mike treated them all to a buffet lunch at the Chinese restaurant in Weaverville.

Everyone loved Sadie, and Sadie especially adored Tyler. When he was present she had eyes for no one else, and had to sit beside him at the table and on the floor at his feet to watch TV. Tyler brought her a tadpole in a jar, a goldfish in a bowl. He enjoyed reading to her.

But now and then, Amelia felt a prick of fear. What if Darren showed up? What if this woman and child, whom she had come to love, were taken from her as Caroline and Thomas had been?

Mother's Day this year would fall on May 13, and they began to plan a picnic for the entire extended family. Hannah's daughter, Miranda, and her husband and sons would be coming from Pennsylvania. They choose Lake Gillian off Long Shoals Road, south of Asheville. Hannah reserved adjoining covered areas with tables and benches. Tyler stayed busy honing his skills in the canoe that his grandfather, Bob, had recently bought him, and Sadie was beside herself, for Tyler had promised to take her canoeing on the lake.

And then, on an afternoon none of them would forget, a black station wagon with dark tinted windows pulled into Max's driveway, and a tall, broad-shouldered man stepped out. For several minutes he leaned against the car, then strolled casually to the edge of Cove Road, shaded his eyes with his hand, and appeared to be studying the ladies' house across the road. Then he strode back to Max's place and rang the front doorbell.

• • •

Anna had been standing at the living-room window, observing his behavior. Immediately, she knew that it was Darren Smith. When he started toward the house, she ran out the back door to fetch Jose. Together, they watched the man ring the doorbell.

"You go answer the door, Jose," Anna whispered. "This man no good. I think he Señora Miriam's husband. Don't let him in the house. Tell him nobody home."

"*Usted debe decirle,*" Jose replied, nudging her toward the door. "I stay behind you."

"*Cobarde*, where is your courage?" She glowered at him, then walked to the door and opened it. "*Sí, señor?*"

"You have a Miriam Smith living here?" His voice was deep and businesslike.

Anna shook her head. "*Lo siento, no comprendo.*" Then she shut the door and locked it. Her entire body shook, and for a moment she clung to Jose. Then she drew herself up. "Jose. Run quick to Señora Grace. Go out back and down by the church. Cross the road by the Herrills. Go along the back of the houses to Señora Grace's kitchen. Tell her to find Señora Miriam and say she no should come home. I call Señor Max and Señora Hannah." She clasped her hands over her heart. "*Dios mio*, where is Sadie?"

"She went to the park with Señor Max this morning." Jose squeezed her hand, and then he slipped out of the kitchen door and motioned for Fortino, his helper, to join him. Moments later they were on their way. When they reached Grace's kitchen, Jose pounded on the door, then dashed from window to window at the rear of the house, knocking.

Grace sat in the rocking chair in the guest room watching television. The moment she spotted Jose at the window, she knew. Her heart racing, she hastened to let him into the kitchen.

Jose appeared frightened as he explained, in broken English, that a man had come to the door asking for Señora Miriam. Anna had pretended not to understand him, and he had gone away.

Grace could hardly think straight. Amelia had left for South Carolina with all her camera equipment early this morning. Where was Miriam? Did Miriam carry a cell phone? Who might have that number? Hannah? For a moment Grace stared blankly at the phone before remembering the number of Bella's Park. The receptionist said Hannah was out in the rose garden with the workmen.

"This is an emergency," Grace said. "Please go and get her. I'll wait."

Jose and Fortino looked at one another, uncertain whether to stay or leave. Grace waved at them. "Go tell Anna I'm trying to locate Miriam, and not to let that man into the house."

She no look good to me, Jose thought. *She look like she gonna fall on the floor. I better wait.* He told Fortino in Spanish, "*Vaya a casa, diga a Ana.*" Fortino nodded and the heavy screen door of the kitchen slammed behind him. "He tell Anna," Jose said. He removed his cap, twisted it in his hands and studied Grace. *Her face red like tomatoes I grow last year. No look good.*

Why was it taking so long for Hannah to come to the phone? Grace's foot tapped the floor and she started to nibble at a fingernail. Then she heard Hannah's voice on the phone.

"Hannah!" Grace repeated what Jose had told her. "I don't know why Anna thought he was Miriam's ex-husband, but she has good instincts. And better safe than sorry. No, I have no idea where Miriam is. Sadie's with you? Good. I hoped you'd know where Miriam was."

Another pause.

"I agree, he could be watching the place. You think he believed Anna, thought it was her house? I doubt that. Why would he choose Max's place and ask for Miriam?" She brought her free hand to her head. "I can't think straight." Grace covered the phone with her palm and turned to Jose. "They want to know what kind of car the man was driving."

Jose stretched his arms sideways. "Long and *negro*, black. Windows *negro*, too."

Grace relayed the information "What did he look like?" she asked Jose.

Jose stood on tiptoe and stretched his arms into the air. "*Grande*, very big." *Good I stayed. She need to know these things.*

"That's a good idea, Hannah. Let Sadie lie on the back seat. You don't want him to catch a glimpse of her. You'll call Mike, and take Sadie to his house? That's right, that's the address. What about clothes?" A pause. "Not even a small suitcase? Yes, yes, I understand. Max will find Miriam." How, she did not ask. "No, I'm fine. Jose's here." She nodded at Jose.

He grinned, pleased that he had stayed.

"Okay." Grace hung up the phone. Suddenly, she felt woozy. Grace reached out and steadied herself against the wall, then placed a finger on a spot between her eyes, as the doctor had instructed her to do if she stood too fast, or got out of bed too hastily and felt dizzy.

"Bring that chair for me, please, Jose? If I don't sit, I may fall."

She look too white now, Jose thought. "You should lie down on couch, Señora Grace. I help you."

Grace accepted his arm and he guided her to the couch in the living room. "We put up your feet." He placed a pillow beneath them, as he had done for his mother in South America and once for Anna, when she was pregnant. "I get cool towel for *cabeza.*" Jose hastened to the kitchen, returned with a cold towel, and placed it across Grace's brow.

"*Gracias*, Jose. Please phone Anna. Ask her to try to find Bob. He may be at the country club in Asheville. She can look up the number in the phone book. When she gets them, she should say that this is an emergency and that Mr. Richardson must call Grace Singleton right away."

"Sí, señora." Moments later, Grace could hear Jose speaking rapidly on the phone in Spanish. Now she could only wait.

Grace closed her eyes.

Sixteen

Miriam

Miriam filled the car with gas and ventured out to explore the countryside west of Asheville. Gradually the landscape changed: pastures grew steeper, houses farther apart, and dramatic mountains overshadowed ever-narrowing valleys.

Miriam left the highway and rambled aimlessly along tree-shaded back roads, past rows of postal boxes planted firmly on high posts at the driveways of nineteen-fifties type bungalows. Turning a corner, she stumbled into the town of Waynesville, nestled in an ample valley ringed by mountains.

Attracted by the charm of Main Street, with its art galleries and gift and antique shops, Miriam wandered from one shop to another. A stunning turquoise-blue silk scarf, perfect for Amelia, caught her eye, and she purchased it. Back in her car, she continued along back roads until she found herself on the shore of a lovely lake. A sign informed her that this was part of a Methodist retirement and retreat center. Upscale homes nestled behind trees and shrubs, while across the lake, a hotel towered above rows of smaller homes. A sailboat on the far side of the lake drifted lazily close to shore. She had stumbled upon the perfect place to enjoy the picnic lunch that Anna had packed for her.

Miriam settled on the grass, her back against a tree trunk, and smiled at the ducks paddling by, leaving a trail of ripples in their wake. She broke the crust of her sandwich into tiny bits, walked to the edge of the grass, and cast the crumbs out onto the water. The ducks whipped about and raced to devour them.

The idyllic weeks in Covington had lulled her into relaxing. Amelia's acceptance, and their growing and mutual affection, were continual sources of joy. Amazingly, other things were falling into place. Brenda Tate had offered her a job as a temp, teaching second grade at Caster Elementary School in the fall. Grace hinted that she, Hannah, and Amelia might build a guesthouse on their land, in which she and Sadie might live if they wanted to. Oh, how she wanted to. At last she and Sadie could be part of a loving extended family.

Miriam stretched out on the grassy slope, brought her arms behind her to rest her head on her hands, and watched the clouds change. She had loved to gaze at the clouds when she was a child, and as she lay peacefully in the grass, pleasant childhood memories drifted through her mind.

On Saturday afternoons the doorbell would ring at four o'clock, and Mrs. Treadwell would arrive for tea and crumpets. Miriam could smell the round, fat crumpets, fresh from the oven, raisins popping through their crusty tops. She'd once asked her mother why Mrs. Treadwell, who walked in and out of their home at will, rang the doorbell on Saturday afternoons.

Her mother pondered this. "Well, Miriam, Saturday tea is a special time that we set aside for relaxation. It's the day when I don't have to go to work, when I own my own time."

"You don't go to work on Sundays," Miriam had said.

"That's true, but there's church on Sundays, and getting ready for Monday. Saturdays are special. I adore Saturday afternoon tea with my best friend and my dear daughter. Now, come along and help me finish setting the table."

Mama reached into the mahogany china cabinet and brought down delicate china teacups and Gran's teapot, while Miriam placed silver spoons and knives, also from Gran, alongside the Irish linen napkins with Mama's initial *S* embroidered in green in the corners. Once the table was set, Mama would put on her favorite ankle-length chiffon dress, and Miriam dressed up, too.

Matilda Treadwell, Tilly, usually wore her graying hair pinned atop her head. But on Saturdays she visited a beauty salon, and arrived for tea with her hair in a wide bun at the nape of her neck. Mrs. Treadwell was an herbalist, and supplemented her pension by selling neatly bundled concoctions of herbs grown in her organic garden. Sometimes she'd bring a small bundle of dried ground herbs with her on Saturdays.

"Try this new tea," she said. "Tell me how you like it. I'm going to call it Love Goes Lightly Tea."

As they sipped it, Mama smiled and commented on how

good the tea was, though it was slightly bitter. But sometimes the tea she brought was delicious, sweet and pleasant.

Smells from the past still stopped Miriam in her tracks. Just yesterday, she had stepped into the kitchen while Anna was chopping herbs, and the smell had reminded her of Mrs. Treadwell.

"What is that you're chopping?" she had asked.

"*Albabaca,*" Anna replied. "Basil."

So that was it! Mrs. Treadwell must have used it so frequently that the scent clung to her hands, her hair, even her clothing.

In the warm sunshine, Miriam soon drifted off to sleep. When she awoke, she checked her watch. It was getting late. Hannah must be worn out with Sadie, who asked a million questions, and she had to drop off some film at Mike's shop in Weaverville for Amelia. Miriam packed up her picnic and headed to her car.

Seventeen

Darren Arrives

After talking to Grace, Hannah stood for a moment feeling totally disoriented. Her heart pounded. This is no time for the fainthearted, she thought, as she collected herself and took a deep breath. Moments later, she dashed from her office to find Max.

Word had spread that Hannah had received an emergency call, and Max was already on his way to her office. They collided in the hallway and stood there for a second holding one another. Max had assumed it could only be one thing: Darren Smith. As they walked to her office, Hannah related Grace's phone call.

"Where's Sadie?" he asked.

"With Wayne in the rose garden. We were cutting out the remaining dead stalks."

He went to her desk and buzzed the receptionist. "Get Wayne and Sadie in here right away, will you? They're in the rose garden." Max joined Hannah on the sofa, placed his arms about her, and held her. His indestructible Hannah was trembling.

"There's so much at stake," she said.

"Because we love them," Max said.

Hannah nodded and rested her head against his chest. A moment later, he rose and went to her desk, this time to dial Mike at his workshop. Mike answered at the second ring. In a terse, quiet voice Max explained the situation, and Mike agreed that they should take Sadie to his home.

"There's a key under the green flowerpot near my front door," Mike said. "And there's plenty of food in the fridge. Help yourselves. As far as I know, Miriam doesn't have a cell phone." Mike's voice sharpened. "Wait—I see her. She's parking outside. I'll get her on the phone."

"No, please. Tell her yourself and then take her to your place. We'll meet you there in a few minutes."

"Agreed," Mike said.

"Anything you need to take care of here before we go?" Max asked Hannah.

"Nothing that can't wait." If there was anything of importance, she couldn't think of what it was.

"Do you need to let Laura know?"

"Not now. I just can't think straight. I'll phone her from Mike's. And Grace—Lord, we ought to stop and get Grace! She's alone in the house. She must be going crazy."

He grabbed the phone. "I'll call and tell her where we're going. She can meet us there. We don't want to hang around Cove Road and risk being seen by Smith. He might be spying on the house."

From the hallway, they could hear Sadie singing.

"She's such a happy child," Hannah said. "And now this. When will it end for them? This will break Amelia's heart."

There was laughter and the door flew open. Sadie, her face flushed, her eyes bright and happy, stood there. "I'm singing a song Wayne just taught me. I learn songs fast."

"She certainly does." Behind her, Wayne winked at them. He wore jeans and a green T-shirt, and his shoulder-length dark hair was windblown. When Hannah had first come to live in Covington, Wayne, a country boy and high school dropout with little more than a green thumb and an unattractive attitude, had worked with her in her greenhouse. She had encouraged him to get his GED, had guided him and financed his education at Haywood Community College, where he studied horticulture. After graduation, she had hired him as her foreman at Bella's Park. He had become, in many ways, the son she never had.

Wayne immediately sensed that something was amiss. "Anything I can do here?" He looked directly at Hannah.

"Maybe get these boxes of plant stakes out of here and unpack them. I'd appreciate that. I ordered tags with the names imprinted on them, so you can have the men go ahead and place them. You may have to show them which stake goes to which plant."

He nodded and started toward the boxes.

"We'll finish the roses when I get back, Wayne, and thank you. I'll phone you." She raised her eyebrows and glanced briefly in Sadie's direction.

A look of concern crossed Wayne's face. "Will do." He hoisted a box on his shoulder and started for the door.

Max scooped up Sadie. "Come on, honey. We're going to meet your mama."

Outside, Hannah stepped into the road to look for any unfamiliar car or person, then motioned Max to join her. Max suggested that Hannah drive. "Sadie and I are gonna play a game and I'll need both hands free."

Sadie giggled when Max instructed her to lie down on the floor of the back seat and pull her sweater over her head. "Now, you're a big old grizzly bear and you're hiding deep in the woods. I'm gonna look and look, and when I find you I'm gonna reach back and tickle you good."

Sadie scrambled into the back seat and scrunched into a ball on the floor, then pulled her sweater over her head and shoulders. Hannah drove down Cove Road and turned right on the back road that would take them to the highway to Weaverville.

Eighteen

The Flight to Roger's Place

Miriam entered Mike's workshop studio. Her heart plummeted when she saw his face.

"Let's go," he said, taking her arm, propelling her out of the door. "Darren's here. He went to Max's house looking for you. Anna pretended not to speak English, and he went away."

Miriam felt her legs giving way. "Oh, my God."

He waited as she leaned against the wall.

"How did she know it was Darren?" she asked.

"Anna's got good instincts. Is he tall and dark-haired, with an attitude about him like he owns you?"

She closed her eyes and wished the pounding in her ears would stop. "Yes, that sounds like him. Darren's found us. Dear Lord, how I've dreaded this moment."

"Max and Hannah took Sadie to my place. I'll drive your car there. I'm glad I changed the license plate on it. You get down low, so if he's somewhere about and sees this car, he won't see you in it."

She hardly dared to breathe as Mike drove to his home, where everyone but Amelia waited. She excused herself, went into the bedroom, and phoned Roger.

"Just come," he said. "Now, don't cry. Time for that later. Be brave. You have the directions. If you get lost, call me. I'll be waiting for you. You can do this, Miriam. You're scared, I know, but keep driving. It's going to be all right."

It hurt that Amelia did not know that she must flee again, or where she was going. They were all afraid, as she was. She could see it in their faces, faces she had come to love and trust, and in their eyes and gestures. Grace and Hannah cried, but they understood and wanted her gone.

In the living room, Sadie clung to Max. "Let me stay with Max and Hannah," she begged.

Max said gently, "It's just for a while. You'll be coming back to us soon." He carried her to the car.

"You promise?" she asked, clutching his arm.

"I promise." He nodded, hoping this would be the case.

They pulled out of the driveway, with Sadie screaming and pounding on the window. It took all Miriam's strength to speak to her daughter quietly and calmly, but she finally managed to calm the child, and Sadie retreated into a hostile silence.

They had been driving for what seemed an endless time, when Miriam realized that she had missed the left turn to Highway 11. Sweat formed on her forehead and her heart raced. What could she do? With all this traffic, where could she turn around? This highway went to Greenville. She would be lost. She would never find Roger's place.

Perspiration slid between her breasts, and she pressed one hand against her chest. *Please, God, help me.*

A car ahead of her pulled into the left lane and made a U-turn across a narrow dirt opening, which she would have driven past and never noticed otherwise. Offering a silent prayer of thanks, she followed the car, turned back the way she had come, and took the turn that Roger described.

Miriam lowered the visor to shade her eyes from the glare of the setting sun. Sadie had fallen asleep, thank goodness, her head lolling to one side, her mouth slightly open. They were fleeing again, with only a bag of clothing she had stored in the trunk of her car, along with the jewelry box containing the last of her mother's valuable jewelry.

But at least this time, she had a destination. Her friend Roger would be waiting. Miriam took a slow, deep breath. There was no need now for either speed or haste.

Sadie stirred. "Where are we going, Mama?"

"To visit Roger."

"Good. I love Roger."

Sadie sat straight, then pulled a candy bar from her purse and offered her mother a bite. Miriam shook her head, and Sadie devoured the candy bar. "I want a drink," she said.

"We'll stop at the first gas station we come to. And Roger will have plenty for us to eat and drink when we get there."

"How far is that?"

"It's not far now."

As she crested a rise, the sun sank. A heaviness that Miriam recognized as a precursor to depression settled about her heart. For Sadie's sake, she must shake off this feeling.

Sadie's voice startled her. "Daddy found us, didn't he, Mama? That's why everyone was so upset, right? That's why we're running away again, isn't it?"

The fear in her daughter's voice was more painful than her own fear. *Damn Darren.* She took a deep breath. "Yes. He found us."

"Did you see him?"

"No. He came to the door of Max's house and asked for us. Anna pretended she didn't speak English and he went away."

"I'm scared, Mama."

"I know, honey, but we're going to Roger. He lives way out in the country, where we'll be safe. Roger will take care of us."

"Will I ever see Anna and Amelia, and Max and Hannah, and Grace and Bob and Tyler again? I really like Tyler . . ." Her voice trailed away, ending the sentence on a quivering note.

"I'm sure you'll see them again. And we'll feel better once we get to Roger's house. We'll have a nice dinner."

"Are you going to marry Roger, Mama?"

Miriam laughed. "No, he's like a brother to me. Let's sing, shall we?"

Sadie immediately perked up. "Yes, I'll sing the song your mama taught you, and you and your friends would hold hands and go round and round singing it."

Waiting for a partner, waiting for a partner.
Go round the ring and pull one in
And kiss her when you get her in.

Miriam joined in, and they drove for a time repeating the refrain.

A sign indicating a four-way stop brought them to a temporary halt. The road dipped, and the sound of the tires grew smoother when they reached a concrete bridge crossing a lake that Roger had mentioned. Sadie pointed to lights from homes that dotted the shoreline.

"They look so pretty, like a diamond necklace," she said.

"It's not much longer to Roger's place." Miriam pulled off the road into a dirt driveway, snapped on the overhead light, and checked the directions. "Keep your eyes open for a big gas station on the right-hand side." She put the paper on the dashboard, and checked for traffic. She would have welcomed the lights of a car to follow on the unfamiliar road, but none appeared, and she pulled back onto Highway 11.

"We'll turn right at that gas station. Then we drive until we come to a hillside cemetery that's on the left. I need you to be my eyes, since I have to keep mine on the road."

"I'll look to the left and right, left and right."

"That's a fine idea, Sadie."

It was a huge relief when the gas station came into view, its tall red and white sign as welcome as a lighthouse's beacon. "Do you still want a drink?" She glanced over at Sadie.

Sadie leaned forward, her eyes lit with excitement, "No. I just want to get to Roger's house."

Miriam's sentiments exactly.

Soon the Alexander Cemetery loomed on the left. "I see it, Mama! What are those white boxes on the hill? They look like steps, but you'd have to jump from one to the other."

"Those are graves. People are buried inside of them."

"Oh." Sadie turned her neck for a last look as they drove past.

• • •

Standing in his doorway, his house ablaze in light, Roger welcomed them with open arms. He lifted Sadie high above his head, and as she descended, she threw her arms about his neck and clung to him as if for dear life. Then he set her down and hugged Miriam. Questions spilled from him faster than Miriam could reply.

"Where is your luggage? Have you eaten dinner? How was the drive? Did you have any trouble finding this place?"

"Only one small suitcase in the boot. No, we haven't had dinner, and no, we didn't have any trouble finding you."

"Come on in, then, and feast yourselves on specially prepared vittles."

She slipped her arm through his, which comforted her, and they went inside.

Sadie headed for the television. "May I watch cartoons, Roger?"

"Certainly. Just click away until you find them; I have no idea what channel cartoons live on." Roger led Miriam across the great room to a door, then down a hall to the guest bedroom. He set her suitcase on a folding stand.

The room was bright and cheerful, with yellow- and rose-colored floral bedspreads and curtains and lemon-yellow walls. A table with two reading lamps separated twin beds with French Provincial headboards. In the corner stood a matching armoire, and Roger opened the center doors, displaying a flat screen television.

"All the doors in this house are made of solid wood, and when you close them, no one in the house can hear the television. Feel free to watch it any time of the day or night."

Huge white-and-yellow carnations spilled from a bowl on a low table beside a rocking chair near one of the windows. Roger went to the window and lowered the blinds. "This room faces east, so the morning light might awaken you early. I do hope you'll be comfortable here."

"I'm sure we'll be very comfortable. It's a lovely, welcoming room." Miriam hugged him. "Thank you, dear Roger, for sheltering us. Thank you from the bottom of my heart."

"No reason to thank me; I think of you as my family. My home is your home." He guided her toward the door. "When Sadie's asleep, we can talk. Come on, you must be famished."

Miriam hesitated, looking about the pleasant but unfamiliar room, which contained none of her possessions: no pictures of herself and Sadie, no slippers tucked beneath the bed, no books stacked on the night table. Just one small suitcase with a few items, and the oppressive reality that yet again, she was starting almost from scratch. There seemed to be no light at the end of this tunnel.

Seeming to sense her hopelessness, Roger held out his hands. "Come, Miriam. You must be exhausted. This isn't a good time to think—just let yourself relax. You're safe here."

A rush of gratitude lightened her sadness. How lucky she was that Roger had come into her life. How fortunate to be here in this house, hidden from sight down a rural, one-lane road in a remote area of South Carolina. If she could hide from Darren anywhere, it would be here.

Nineteen

Amelia Returns

Amelia's photo workshop in Greenville focused on the restored downtown Main Street and the Reedy River's newly unveiled waterfall, which for decades had been hidden beneath an ugly bridge that spanned the river. The removal of the old bridge and accumulated debris revealed a waterfall that took one's breath away.

At lunch Amelia began to feel uneasy, as if something were wrong at home. She mentioned it to her photo partner.

"I get like that whenever I'm away from home," the woman said. "I think it's because we're women and so much depends on us. We think we need to be home to handle everything that might come up."

"You're probably right." Although she was tempted to phone Mike, Amelia decided against it and threw herself into her work.

The workshop ended at two in the afternoon and Amelia headed back up the mountain. Since she was no longer concentrating on photography, her mind finally succumbed to the anxiety that had been nagging at her all afternoon, and by the time she pulled into the driveway of their home, her palms were sweating.

The note pinned to her pillow upstairs confirmed the worst. For a long while, Amelia stood at her bedroom window and stared down at Cove Road. The wind whipped the week-old dogwood blossoms from their stems; they fell to earth, ringing the tree trunks with drifts of white. She imagined Max's front door opening and Sadie, bright eyed and happy, running to the edge of the road, stopping to look both ways as she had been taught to do, then hurrying across the road to visit her.

The sky was blue, the sun shone, and a cruel fate had whisked that precious child and her mother away from her. Would she ever see them again? Weeping, Amelia turned from the window. The stillness of the silent house seemed to overlay her very being.

She shuffled to the closet, slowly unbuttoned her blouse, and placed it on a hanger. Sitting on the edge of the bed, she removed her shoes and slipped her feet into the comfortable furry slippers Grace had given her last Christmas. She stood, allowed her skirt to fall, and stepped out of the puddle it formed about her feet. She could not remember when she had felt so old and so tired. After a moment, she reached down and picked up the phone to call Mike. On the other end, Hannah answered.

"I am so sorry, Amelia. They've been gone about an hour. We're all still here, in shock. Yes, Darren is in town, somewhere in the area." Hannah explained about Anna and Darren, and that Miriam and Sadie had left. There had been no time to think or talk. No one knew where she was headed.

"I might have driven right past her on the highway," Amelia said, her voice cracking.

"Maybe, maybe not. I have no idea what road she took. No, don't come over. We're leaving now to come home. Are you all right?"

"No. I don't think that I'll ever be all right again."

"Don't think like that, Amelia. Grace and I will be home soon."

The phone fell from Amelia's trembling hand and clattered as it struck the floor. She moved to the window, lowered the blind, and drew the curtains, then she took her robe from a hook inside the closet and slipped into it. *Oh God, help me.* What would she do? She loved them. She hadn't loved anyone like this since Caroline died.

Amelia threw herself on her bed and sobbed.

Grace and Hannah found Amelia curled in a ball in the center of her bed. Empty now of tears, she looked at them with anguished eyes.

"There was always the risk that he would find her, that Miriam would have to run from him," Hannah said. "We all knew that."

"I don't need you to tell me that. It doesn't change anything, and it doesn't help," Amelia said.

"Sorry." Hannah gave Grace a quick glance, turned, and left the room.

"I'm sorry if I hurt her feelings. I find her so insensitive sometimes," Amelia said. She covered her heart with her hand. I let myself love them, allowed myself to believe they would be with me forever. Miriam loved it here. She wanted to make Covington her home." Tears rose in her eyes again. "I loved them so much."

Grace stretched out on the bed beside her friend and took Amelia's hand in hers. They lay without speaking for a long while. Then Grace realized that Amelia's breathing had quieted. She had fallen asleep.

Twenty

THE PLAN

Earlier, after the shock of Darren's arrival in Covington, and after Miriam and Sadie had driven away, and before Amelia had returned from her workshop, no one at Mike's had seemed able to speak. Max and Bob wandered aimlessly about Mike's living room, while Mike set platters of cold cuts and bread and a pitcher of iced tea on the dining room table. But no one had any appetite.

Finally, Grace said, "We should call the police and tell them about Darren—what he did to Miriam."

Bob placed his arm about her and drew her close. "I've talked to the chief of police over in Mars Hill and told him everything we know. He said that without a crime, they can't arrest him."

"He has to *kill* her before they can arrest him?" Hannah's voice had never sounded so shrill.

"We could tell him that Miriam and Sadie have never been here," Mike suggested, but Max reminded them that many other people in Covington knew Miriam or Sadie.

Eventually, Max suggested that they acknowledge that Miriam and Sadie had indeed been living in Covington, and that they were on a Caribbean cruise and wouldn't be back for two weeks.

"That'll give her time to put a lot of distance between here and wherever she's going," Max said. He punched a fist into the palm of his other hand. "Confound it! I wish we'd talked about this, wish we knew if she had a plan or a place in mind. She could be headed anywhere. We must stop him from going after her, for a while at least."

"Not the Caribbean. It's too easy to get there," Grace said. "Make it Alaska."

"We could suggest that he hang out in Covington, then show him around, keep him busy. That way we can keep our eyes on him," Max said.

Hannah hit Max on the arm. "That's the stupidest thing I ever heard."

"You got a better idea?" He rubbed his arm.

Hannah shook her head and kissed his cheek. "I'm sorry. The thought of you having to spend time with that bastard chills me through and through."

But another half hour of discussion had produced no better idea, and Max's plan prevailed.

Twenty-one

The Personification of Evil

When Darren showed up again at Max's place, Hannah opened the door and introduced herself. As planned, she told him that Miriam and Sadie had been in Covington, and that they were away on a cruise to Alaska and would return in two weeks. She led him to the barn, where Max was working. They invited Darren inside the house for coffee and sat through a long, sometimes incoherent tale of woe, in which he assured them that he was a reformed man, in love with his wife, and desperately wanted to be reunited with his family. They played the fool and suggested that he check into the new motel on Elk Road, where he could wait for her return. Darren considered that briefly and decided that was exactly what he would do.

When he was gone, Hannah said, "I *hate* him. He's a liar, a horrible man. Did you notice his eyes, how he doesn't look directly at you? He's evil." She shuddered.

Max and Bob assumed the task of entertaining Darren and keeping a close eye on his goings and comings. To their disgust, they soon discovered that along with his volatility and potential for violence, the man was a loathsome drunk.

On his second day in Covington, at breakfast at Poppy's Restaurant in Weaverville, Darren pulled a silver flask from his pocket and took a long swig. From its smell, Max and Bob judged it to be strong whiskey.

Max couldn't help thinking of Johnny Cash's song "Sunday Morning Going Down." The man in the song says that he's had a drink for breakfast and is considering yet another drink for "dessert." It was obvious that regardless of the time of day or night, Darren consumed many desserts.

The man was foulmouthed, incapable of finishing a sentence without using gutter language. Max wondered how much of this Sadie had been exposed to, and why Miriam had tolerated this monster for as long as she had.

The first incident wasn't long in coming. At the mall, a drunken Darren staggered into an older woman, knocking her to the floor. The woman struck and cut her head, and lay there bleeding. When her husband asked for Darren's name and address and the name of his insurance company, Darren went ballistic. He cursed the man and accused the man's wife of having bumped into him.

Fortunately, another shopper had witnessed the incident and used his cell phone to call the police. An ambulance took the woman and her husband to the hospital, and the police arrested Darren. At the station they charged him with battery and unruly conduct, and called Bob.

The policeman told him, "This guy's got a record of

abuse. He did time for violating two restraining orders, you know that?"

"I do. We're trying to keep him here for a few days, so that his ex-wife can put as much distance between them as possible," Bob explained.

"I wish her good luck. I could lock him up for a couple of days, if you prefer not to post bail."

Bob wanted to let Darren sit in jail, but Max reminded him that Darren could find bail through a bondsman and be out and gone, heaven knew where. It was best, they decided, to bail him out and keep him in sight. Bob posted bail, and drove the drunken Darren back to the motel in Covington.

"What was I gonna do?" Bob asked Grace when she upbraided him for posting bail.

"Let him sit in jail and rot. You'll never see that money."

Bob scratched his head. "I tell you, he'd have gotten the money from a bondsman, and gotten out and been gone. Max and I are gonna keep a close eye on him until the court date."

Darren's drinking fed the monster in him. Several days after the mall incident, Max found Jose crouched in a corner of the barn, his head in his hands, blood oozing through his fingers.

"Good Lord, Jose, what happened to you?" Max helped Jose to his feet.

"Señor Smith. He come in the barn. He call me stupid Mexican, a wetback. He say I must go back to Mexico, I can no stay in America. I try to tell him I have green card. He no listen."

"You're bleeding. Did you fight with him?"

"No, I no fight. He fight me."

Max helped him to the kitchen, where Anna's eyes went hard as granite. She wiped his forehead clean, and laid a ice-cold compress across his head. "This why we left Mexico. This is what gangsters there do to good people who no sell cocaine."

"I try to show him my green card, but *el me empujó*—he shove me against the barn door, then he shove me on the ground and kick me." Jose pointed to his side, and Max's rage mounted at the imprint of a dirty shoe on Jose's shirt. "I tell him I make American citizen next month, but he no listen." He made a sign with his finger against his temple, indicating that Darren was crazy. "He *loco.*"

"Damn him," Max said. "*Loco* is right."

Max waited until Anna had soothed and bandaged her husband, and they left the kitchen for their apartment in the back. Then he raced to his SUV and tore down the road to the motel. Max banged on Darren's door, and when Darren opened it, Max grabbed him by the shoulders and shook him hard. He shoved Darren into the room and pinned him to a wall.

Suddenly, Max realized that his hands were at Darren's throat. He pulled away.

"Don't you *ever* go near my barn, or speak to or touch Jose, Fortino, or Anna. Do you understand me?" He towered over Darren, who lay cowering on the bed, staring at Max through bloodshot, blurry eyes. "You keep off my property or I'll have you arrested!"

Shaking, Max stormed from the room, hating himself for having lost control and stooping to Darren's level.

"I'm done with it, with him. He can fry in hell," he told Hannah when he got home.

Frightened for him, for his health, his blood pressure, she held his trembling body close. In a flash, she remembered that she, too, could hate another person so intensely that she would want to kill him. The thought, and the emotions that accompanied it, frightened Hannah, who considered herself a peaceful person, someone who settled disagreements calmly through compromise and negotiation. Yet, here she was wishing that she could destroy Darren—for Miriam's sake, for Sadie's, for all their sakes.

But the worst was yet to come. Three nights later, Bob jolted awake to a ringing phone. Once again, it was the police.

"Sorry to be calling you this late, Mr. Richardson. This is Sergeant Briggs over in Marshall. You know a fellow by the name of Darren Smith? He gave us your name. Said to call you and you'd get him a lawyer and bail him outta jail."

"What's he done this time?" Bob's heart began to race.

"He was out at the Ole Boys Bar on the Marshall highway. It's a rough place. Smith was drinking heavily, and he called some fellow a sissy and a girly man. The guy took a swing at him, and Smith went crazy, is what everyone says. He pitched a chair at the bartender and broke his hand, then smashed a bottle of whiskey on some guy's head. The ole fellow's over at Mission Hospital emergency gettin' stitches. Those guys who hang out at that bar are pretty tough, but they say this Smith fellow was swinging and cussing like a devil. He pulled a knife on some fellow, and a bunch of them jumped him and pinned him down until we could get there. Said they'd never seen a man go crazy like that, at the snap of a finger."

Bob refused to bail him out. *We agreed that we would keep him here, for Miriam's sake*, he thought. *The two weeks are nearly up. Then I don't care what he does or what happens to him.*

By the next day, Darren had indeed found a bondsman and was out on the street again.

"I tell you, Bob." Max turned to him. It was the next day and they were driving to the motel on Elk Road, where Darren was staying. "Despite everything we've been through, I still believe that it's best to keep the enemy close."

"In all my years in the army I've seen some pretty rough people, but I never met a man with so much venom in him. Darren Smith is one hell of a loathsome creature," Bob said.

Max parked his SUV in the motel lot next to Darren's car with its dark windows. "He's cutting into my life," Max said. "I'm way behind with my paperwork for the dairy, and we've got heifers that have to go to auction. Hannah's handling the load for both of us at Bella's Park. Everyone's under a lot of stress."

"You can say that again. Grace is a nervous wreck. She keeps asking me what we're gonna tell him when Miriam doesn't come back."

Max turned off the engine, sat back, and rubbed his chin. "Tell you the truth, I haven't a clue, Bob."

"After what's been going on, Grace is convinced that Darren's going to turn violent when we tell him the truth, and maybe come after one of us."

"We could tell him that Miriam phoned a friend here, and when she heard Darren was in town, she decided not to come back," Max said.

Bob swung about to face Max. "That's a great idea! Then he can pack up and go off on his own wild-goose chase."

"After he gets good and drunk and goes nuts again. Maybe we can alert the cops ahead of time and they'll be on the lookout for him. Hopefully, by then, Miriam will have found a safe haven," Max replied.

"Okay, so what do we do with him today?" Bob asked.

"Get him out of town, away from decent people, someplace where he can't get a drink. I thought we'd take him fishing down at Lake James."

"Sounds good," Bob said.

"What the devil? You're drunk," Max said, when Darren staggered down the walk, stumbled over the curb, and slumped against the SUV.

"Who's drunk? Not meee. Maybe you guys oughtta get your eyes checked," Darren slurred. He fumbled with the door handle, laboriously hoisted himself into the vehicle, and collapsed on the back seat. His head fell forward, and he began to snore.

"Let's not waste the trip to Lake James," Bob said. "Park him in my driveway, if you prefer, and let him sleep it off. I could use some time off from babysitting this piece of crap!"

"Good idea," Max said.

Three hours later, Max looked up from his desk. "I'd better call Bob and check on Darren," he muttered.

When Bob went out to check, Darren had vanished. "Where the devil has he gone to?" Bob asked.

No one had an answer.

Jose shook his head. "I no see him, Señor Max. He no come near the barn or me or Fortino, since you tell him stay away."

Pastor Denny Ledbetter, who had just returned from his daily run, had not seen Darren anywhere.

The ladies noticed nothing amiss at Max's place, or at Bella's Park, where Hannah had been busy laying out the oriental garden with Wayne all morning.

Max said, "Perhaps Darren's staggered off and collapsed in someone's back yard." He visited all their neighbors. Charlie Herrill and Frank Craine shook their heads and joined in the search. The three men walked the perimeter of their houses and a little ways into the woods behind their homes, but Darren was nowhere to be found.

At their request, the motel clerk checked his room and reported that it was empty. "No, sir, he's not been back here since he left with you this morning," the young man said.

Darren's car had disappeared from the motel parking lot. "Well, what next?" Max asked.

"The devil with him," Bob said. "I'm going home."

"If we're lucky, he met the devil and was taken straight to hell, where he belongs. Wouldn't that be a blessing?" Max slapped Bob on the back, and the men set off toward their respective homes.

• • •

The following morning, Max worked with Jose arranging for the shipment of heifers. At noon he settled into his recliner, flipped on the local news, and picked up his newspaper. That afternoon he planned to work with Hannah at Bella's Park. A new road was going in to allow tour buses to take their passengers directly up the hill to the Covington Homestead.

Suddenly a news brief came on, and the reporter's words caught Max's attention. His head jerked up and his newspaper fell to the floor. The screen showed a car standing nearly upright in the Swannanoa River, its front half submerged in the murky water, its rear reaching to the sky.

"The car has Connecticut license plates," the reporter said.

The license plates filled the screen, then the reporter returned. "The sole occupant, a man, carried no identification. He was taken to Mission Memorial Hospital, where he was pronounced dead. If anyone has any information concerning the identity of this man or the car, please call . . ."

Max memorized the number at the bottom of the screen, then switched off the television, shock and relief sweeping through him. Darren was dead. "That's too darn good to be true," he said aloud.

He stood and walked to the window. For a few moments he remained there, then he went to the phone.

"Bob, did you see the news flash on the noon news? That *was* Darren's car, right? Yeah, what a shock! What a relief. Can't say I'm sorry. Sure, I'll call the police in Asheville. They'll probably want us to come in and identify him. Awful as it sounds, it couldn't happen to a better fellow."

The front door opened and Hannah entered. "Max, have

you had lunch yet? I have an errand in Mars Hill. Want to go with me and we'll have lunch?" She stopped in the doorway of the living room. "What's the matter, honey? You look pale as a ghost. What's happened?"

"I think Miriam's problems are permanently over," Max said.

"What do you mean?"

"Darren's car was found in the Swannanoa River this morning. He's dead, Hannah."

"Dead? He drowned? Was it an accident, did they say?"

"A one-car accident. They'll probably do an autopsy to determine the cause of death. The way he drank, maybe he just ran off the road—or maybe he had a stroke or a heart attack. He had no identification on him, and they're asking anyone who recognized the car to contact the police. I was just about to call the Asheville police."

"I guess you'll have to go in and identify him. Do you want me to go with you?"

"Bob's gonna go with me. Darren was drunk out of his mind yesterday, last we saw him. He fell asleep in my car and we left him to sleep it off in Bob's driveway. When Bob went to check on him, he was gone, as was his car from the motel."

"He was a miserable, no-good son of a gun. I can't say I'm sorry," Hannah said. "I'll go tell Grace and Amelia."

"Sure wish we knew where Miriam was." Max walked her to the door.

"So do I. If we could find her, she could come home. It would be so nice for Amelia to have them at our Mother's Day picnic at Lake Julian. But that's just two days away."

• • •

"We have to go tell Amelia," Hannah said, after she reported the news to Grace.

They started up the stairs, Grace leading the way. "I wish we could locate Miriam. I can't bear to think how worried and frightened she is. Now he's dead, and she doesn't even know."

Amelia sat in her chair by the window. She did not turn to greet them.

"We have good news!" Grace reached for Amelia's hand.

Amelia's eyes were red from crying. "What kind of good news?"

"Darren is dead," Hannah announced. "The police found him inside his car, which was facedown in the Swannanoa River in Asheville."

Amelia gasped. "*What?*" Her eyes, which had been dull and listless, sprang to life. "He's *dead?* He's *really dead?*" Her ashen cheeks turned rosy, and she smiled. "I shouldn't be happy about anyone dying, but I'm *so* very happy. Now Miriam and Sadie can come home!"

Amelia's brow furrowed. "But how will she find out? It could be weeks until she contacts us. Oh, we *must* find her." Amelia half rose from her chair, then sat back heavily. "But we can't, can we? We have to wait until she feels safe enough to get in touch with us. Soon, I pray."

Twenty-two

Long Sad Days

To ensure Miriam's safety, Roger avoided contacting his mother for fear he might inadvertently let something slip, opening the door to Darren's tracking her down.

Miriam, cut off from news of Covington, struggled unsuccessfully against depression. Night after night, after the dinner dishes were washed and put away, she retreated to the silence of her bedroom. Sitting in the rocker or lying on her bed, she listened to the lighthearted laughter of her daughter as she and Roger played Monopoly or dominoes. She could not think clearly, could not make a plan, could see no escape from the horror that was Darren. Many nights she hardly slept, and would sit out on the porch and watch the stars circle the heavens. They reminded her of herself, going around in circles.

She turned down Roger's invitations to lunch at the Steak House in Walhalla, to explore the government fish farm, to visit antique stores, to go for a ride in the country. Sadie went and loved each excursion while Miriam enjoyed seeing her daughter happy, she also found herself envying the child's ability to throw herself into activities, to go on living, when she so often felt so dead inside. She even refused to join Sadie and Roger when they walked down to the garden to weed the fledging plants or when they drove into Seneca to the feed and seed store.

At the end of the second week, Roger rented a pontoon boat, packed a picnic lunch, and coaxed Miriam to join them on a trip to the lovely mountain Lake Jocassee.

The lake was calm, the mountains surrounding it the fresh green of spring. They donned life jackets and settled into the boat, and Roger motored along the shore, showing them the waterfalls that fed the lake.

Sadie had never seen a waterfall. She leaned against the boat railing and stared up, trying to follow the tumbling trail of water in its descent. "Does the water come down in one straight shoot, or does it go plunk plunk, plunk over the rocks like steps?" she asked.

"Some of both, I imagine." He tousled her hair, and she smiled up at him.

"I wish I could sit on those rocks and let the water pour over me. Do people ever climb on the rocks?" Sadie pointed at the boulders that bordered the lake, where the water flowed more slowly.

Roger put his arm about her shoulders. "We can't climb on the rocks, but we can drift here for a while. Are we ready for our picnic, do you think?"

"Yes, I'm starving," Sadie replied, leaning farther over the railing.

"It's just eleven, Sadie—we just had breakfast. You can't be hungry," Miriam said. "And don't lean over that rail. Get over here now, and sit down."

Reluctantly, Sadie pushed away from the rail and shuffled over to where her mother sat. "I can't see the top of the waterfalls from here." Sadie craned her neck to the side and looked up.

"You've already seen the top. Now, stop pestering Roger." She looked at Roger. "Roger, let's move on, shall we?"

Roger turned his attention to steering the boat, and they eased out onto the deeper water of the lake.

Except for the purr of the pontoon boat's engine and the occasional roar of a speedboat zipping across the lake, they traveled in silence.

Miriam knew that she was being hard on her daughter, unreasonable even, yet she found her irritation with things in general hard to control. Roger was kind, thoughtful, and it was clear that he enjoyed having them here, but how long could she sit and do nothing? And the separation from Amelia, who had become her surrogate mother and a grandmother to Sadie, was hard to handle. She longed to be back in Covington, with all the wonderful people who had embraced them.

Roger looked at her. "Can Sadie come over here and hold this wheel for a second? That's all she has to do, stand here and keep this wheel in one position."

"Please, Mama?" Sadie asked.

"Well, all right. If you keep a close eye on her, Roger."

"I certainly will."

They exchanged places then, Sadie standing at the rear of the boat, holding on to the steering wheel and Roger sitting beside Miriam. "I know you're hurting, honey. I know you miss the ladies, especially Amelia—so I propose that I call Amelia and tell her where you are. She could easily make a trip down here, telling the others it's to do her photography. You'd feel better if you could see her, talk to her, wouldn't you? Besides, we need to find out if Darren's gone, or what."

"But I'm so afraid. What if Amelia tells someone?"

"She won't, Miriam. I'll talk to her. I'll call my mother to check on her, and I'll ask to speak to Amelia, to see how she's doing. She's probably as devastated and miserable as you are. Why should you both feel this way? I can't stand to see you so unhappy. You've lost weight and there are dark circles under your eyes. I want to see you happy and smiling again."

Tears finally came, and Roger held Miriam as she cried into his shoulder. When she pulled away, he handed her his handkerchief.

"I didn't want Sadie to see me go to pieces like this," she sniffed.

"Look at her. She's proud to be entrusted with the wheel, and will probably remember this all of her life. And she's a smart little girl, Miriam. She knows what's going on and she misses everyone, too. When we're alone, she talks about them all the time."

"Okay. Phone Amelia. But if Darren is still around, and if he's threatening them, and she thinks it's not safe for her to come here, tell her not to. I don't want her endangered on my account."

"Don't worry. Amelia's got a good head on her shoulders.

Now, for the rest of the day, just sit back and relax and enjoy your daughter, and our picnic. It's a lovely day. You're as safe as you can possibly get out here on the lake."

"It *is* a nice day." She clasped his hand. "You've done so much for us. How can I thank you?"

"You can begin by drying your tears and enjoying today."

As Roger started back toward Sadie and the wheel, he pulled his cell phone from his back pocket and dialed Covington. The phone rang and rang, then Amelia's voice said, "Hello."

"Amelia, that you? Hi, Roger here. How are you?" There was a pause. "What? What did you say? Really?" Miriam heard his voice rise with excitement. "That's incredible good news! I've never heard better!" Roger turned and walked toward her, his face bright and happy. "Let me tell Miriam. She's right here. I'll tell her, then I'll put her on."

He sat beside her on the bench. "Miriam. Darren drove his car headfirst into the Swannanoa River. He's dead."

She stared at him, her face blank. As the news slowly registered, her face brightened and she smiled. "Is it really true? They know this for sure?"

"Max and Bob identified his body. It's true. You won't have to run and hide ever again."

"Thank God." Miriam's whole body trembled.

"Here, speak to Amelia." Roger handed her the phone.

"Amelia!" Miriam began to cry.

"Don't cry, my sweet child. We've all been through hell, but it's over now. We didn't know how to find you, where to call. I've been frantic with worry."

"I've been with Roger. I've been so miserable, though, I haven't been much company for him. He's as patient as a saint."

"Roger's a good man. Thank God you're safe. Come home soon. How is my Sadie girl?"

"She's great. We're on a pontoon boat on Lake Jocassee. Sadie's steering the boat and Roger's right beside her." She paused, listening intently for a minute. "I want to tell her first, then we'll call you back, and she can talk to you. She's missed you so much, Amelia." A pause again, then, "*I* missed you so much. I love you."

"I love you, too," Amelia said, "with all my heart. What an amazing gift and blessing this is for me. Do you know what tomorrow is?"

"I've lost all track of time. What is it?"

"Mother's Day."

"Mother's Day? Isn't that *grand.* We'll be able to come home for Mother's Day! Is there still going to be a picnic at Lake Julian?"

"Yes, so hurry home," Amelia said. "I'll wait at the house for you, and we'll go to the picnic together."

At the steering wheel, Sadie said, "Look, Roger, Mama's smiling. She looks happy. Who is she talking to?"

"Run over there and she'll tell you. I'll be along in a minute." Alone in this part of the lake and far enough from shore, Roger cut the engine and let the boat drift. Then he followed Sadie to where Miriam waited for her child with outstretched arms.

"Sadie, love, I have something to tell you."

"Mama, your eyes are smiling. Are we going home to

Covington? Is that the news?" She climbed onto the seat beside Miriam.

Miriam took a deep breath and circled Sadie in her arms. "It's about your father, honey."

"Has he gone away and won't come back?" Sadie crossed her fingers and looked at her mother, her eyes filled with hope.

"Why, that's exactly right. He *is* gone, and he won't ever be back. Not *ever.*" Miriam looked up at Roger. Her eyes asked, "Now what?"

Roger kneeled in front of Sadie, who, seeing his expression, grew serious.

"Your daddy had a car accident, honey. A very serious accident."

Sadie nodded. "Mama always said he'd kill himself, driving crazy like he did."

"That's exactly what happened, Sadie. He was driving too fast. His car went off the road and he died."

No one moved or spoke. Water lapped the side of the boat as the wake of a distant boat rocked their pontoon boat.

Sadie looked from Roger to her mother. "Mama, are you all right?" she asked, setting her fingers on her mother's cheek.

Miriam took her daughter's small, soft hand in her own, brought it to her lips, and kissed it. "Yes, I'm fine. We can go home to Covington, to people who love us."

"I don't feel sad. I was frightened of my daddy; he was bad to us." She flung her arms about Miriam. "I'm happy, too, Mama. No one will ever hit you again."

They hugged one another, and Roger moved back to the stern of the boat. He started the engine and turned the pontoon boat toward the dock.

Twenty-three

Happy Mother's Day

Within an hour after the TV news identified Darren Smith's body, the phone at the ladies' home began to ring.

"God forgive me," Velma Herrill said, "but when I heard the news, my heart about jumped out of my chest for joy. He was such a bad one, you wonder why God sent someone like him to this earth. But now he's gone, and your Miriam can come home."

"We haven't a clue where she is," Hannah replied.

"We have a prayer circle at church, and I'll have us all praying for Miriam and Sadie's safe return to Covington."

"We appreciate that," Hannah said.

"Prayer is powerful," Velma said.

Alma Craine echoed those sentiments. "Frank and I just about fell out of our chairs, we were so glad for you all, especially Amelia. Poor thing, she's had such a hard time of it, hasn't she? Do you ladies know where that poor young woman and her child are?"

"We don't know. We hope she'll contact us soon. Miriam and Sadie are very special and dear to us," Grace said.

"Well, we'll be praying for their safe return," Alma said.

"We appreciate that, Alma." Grace set the phone on its hook and turned to Hannah. "I know Alma means well and she's basically good-hearted, but she's such an awful gossip. She's like a turned-on faucet and there's no one to turn her off. I don't think she can stop herself."

"Leave the phone off the hook; let it ring busy for a while," Hannah said. "It hasn't stopped all morning. Lurina called, and said she did a little jig when she heard the news. Laura called, and Brenda and Ellie, and Pastor Denny. He sounded happy, but wasn't too effusive since he's a preacher. Bernice, Ida, June, and May McCorkle all phoned. They said they were darn happy that Mr. Smith got his just deserts, and good riddance to bad rubbish. I haven't heard that expression in years." Hannah poured herself another cup of coffee. "Now, if we could only hear from Miriam."

A whoop came from upstairs. Alarmed, Grace and Hannah turned toward the door. Feet pounded down the stairs, and Amelia dashed into the room, her face pink and animated. "They're coming home! Miriam and Sadie are fine, and they'll be here tomorrow, for Mother's Day. Can you believe it? Mother's Day!" She grinned and said coyly, "You'll never guess where they've been."

"Thank God they're safe and coming home," Grace said. She went to Amelia and hugged her.

"So tell us, where are they?" Hannah asked.

"They've been with Roger, in Salem. All this time, they've been right down the highway."

"Of course. Why didn't I think of that?" Grace said. "When Roger was here, he and Miriam became very good friends."

"How did you find out?" Hannah asked.

"Roger called. Miriam's been so down in the dumps, he thought it might help if she talked to me. I told them about Darren being dead, and Miriam and Sadie are coming home! I am so happy, I could just fly out of that window."

"Our picnic will be a grand celebration" Grace said.

"Let's get on with it, then," Hannah said.

"We'll need a cake and bright tablecloths and napkins." Grace hugged Hannah and Amelia. "I'm about to burst, I am so happy!"

"Well, if Amelia flies off and you burst, I'll have no help with this picnic, So let's sit down and make a list," Hannah said, and they did just that.

On Mother's Day, Amelia awoke to a pristine, clear morning. She loved the month of May, for it marked the end of winter. No longer would she have to bundle up, and the world would brighten with flowers.

But this May was different and she would remember it for the rest of her life. Miriam and Sadie were coming home, and her family—the family she had dreamed of and longed for—would be reunited.

From downstairs, Hannah's voice called to Grace.

Then the front door opened and closed, and Bob's voice floated upstairs. "Max and I'll go ahead and make sure the tables and benches are clean and ready for you gals. Have you heard when Miriam is coming?"

"By noon, I would imagine," Grace said.

Upstairs, Amelia flung back the covers, eased up and got out of bed to stretch out her stiffness, as she did every morning. Usually she lay in bed and lifted and lowered her legs, then pulled them in and straightened them. She'd raise and lower her arms and rotate her ankles. Her osteopath, Dr. Franklin, said that she had a touch of arthritis in her shoulder and hip, and stretching helped, as did a nice hot soak in the bathtub at the end of a day of photography.

Today she wanted to feel as spry and agile as possible. She wished she were fifty, and could scoop Sadie up and hug her as Roger did. Well, she could hug and love Sadie just as much from a sitting position.

Hannah called up the stairs. "You awake, Amelia?"

"I sure am, and I'm getting dressed," Amelia called back.

"We're going ahead, then," Grace said. Dear sweet Grace, without whose loving friendship and wise, comforting words she would never have made it through the days since Miriam and Sadie vanished from her life.

Amelia opened her bedroom door and went to the top of the stairs. Hannah and Grace stood near the front door, picnic baskets in hand. A bright blue and white tablecloth was draped across Grace's arm.

"If there's anything else you need, call and I'll bring it," Amelia said. "See you soon."

Hannah waved, and they walked out the door. Moments later, Hannah's car engine started, then her tires ground on the freshly laid gravel, and they were gone.

• • •

The minutes seemed like hours. Amelia completed her toilette, pulled her soft white hair into a loose bun at the nape of her neck, smoothed foundation on her face, color on her cheeks, and a dab of lipstick. There! No, something was missing. She added her grandmother's tiny pearl earrings. One day she would give them to Miriam. She smiled, satisfied at the thought, and at the way she looked. The light in her eyes alone was enough to brighten her face.

With her eye on the clock, Amelia had a light breakfast, then went out to the porch to wait. Rocking would soothe her and help her contain her excitement.

It wasn't long before Miriam's car turned into the driveway. The catch in Amelia's throat made speech impossible. She stood and waited beside the rocking chair, her arms outstretched, and they ran to her and threw themselves into her embrace.

She held them close, and an invisible circle of love, hope, and gratitude formed about them. Then Sadie wiggled from between them. "You'll smother me, Grandmother," she said.

"Grandmother," Amelia whispered with a sense of wonder.

Miriam nodded. "If you'll have us for a daughter and granddaughter."

Amelia sank into a chair. "Dear God in heaven, thank you. Thank you!"

Miriam kneeled beside her and placed two thornless roses from Roger's garden, one peach and one white, in Amelia's hand. "I didn't have time to buy you a real Mother's Day gift."

Sadie stood behind her chair and ran her fingers softly across Amelia's hair. "The white rose is from me."

"My dear child." Amelia swallowed hard, fighting back tears of joy. "Thank you so much. I love you. You are the answer to the longing of my lifetime, to have a family—a daughter, a granddaughter."

"Let me put them in a vase for you, Grandmother." Sadie took the roses and ran inside.

Miriam reached for Amelia's hand and kissed it, then embraced Amelia. "Happy Mother's Day."

Her arm curved around Miriam, Amelia looked up at the sky. "Thank you, too, Thomas. Thank you, wherever you are."

Discussion Questions

1. Imagine the shock to Amelia when Miriam introduces herself. Close your eyes and consider what you would have felt in Amelia's place. Would you have reacted as she did?

2. What are other ways Amelia might have reacted?

3. The author introduces Miriam's abusive ex-husband. How do you feel about the way Max and Bob handle him when he arrives? What else might they have done?

4. Change occurs slowly for Amelia as she goes through many of the stages of grieving: denial, anger, depression, and finally acceptance. Do you feel that her change of attitude toward Miriam occurred in an appropriate and realistic time frame?

Pocket Books

invites you to enter the world of . . .

JOAN MEDLICOTT

All available from Pocket Books

Turn the page for selections from some of her previous titles. . . .

THE SPIRIT OF COVINGTON

Winds of Change

At midnight on August 2, the wind slackened, then stirred. Gusts sent leaves scurrying. A tiny spark from a cigarette, casually tossed by eighteen-year-old Brad Herrill returning home from a party, flared to life among dry leaves and snaked toward the woods. In the farmhouses fronting the woods on Cove Road, men, women, and children slept.

By two A.M., a necklace of gold edged the outer fringe of trees, and by three A.M. it had crawled into the woods. Heat from the fire sucked moisture from tree trunks. Bursts of wind stirred the flames, causing widening bands of them to veer across pastures, toward barns and farmhouses. In their stalls, cows and horses snorted and pawed the earth, and still the occupants of the houses slept.

In the farmhouse, Amelia Declose awakened. Through her front window George Maxwell's dairy farm across the road shimmered in an eerie, golden glow in a moonless night. When she raised her window, the caustic smell of smoke filled her nostrils. Smoke drifted into her room and set the battery-powered alarm on her wall jangling. From Elk Road, the main road through the hamlet of Covington, fire trucks rounded the corner and tore down Cove Road, their sirens wailing. With increasing panic, Amelia watched the line of trucks: four, five, six. Lights came on in Maxwell's farmhouse.

Amelia screamed.

Within seconds her housemates, Grace Singleton and Hannah Parrish, were at her side.

"A fire, where?" Grace asked, suddenly fully awake.

Amelia stared wild-eyed and pointed toward the window.

"I'm going outside, see where it is," Hannah declared. Moments later, she saw that one of the other farmhouses was ablaze and another spitting flames. Upstairs her housemates were huddled at Amelia's window. "The Herrills' place is on fire, and looks like the Craines' is also," Hannah called.

"What should we do?" Grace shouted to Hannah.

"Get dressed!" Hannah dashed back upstairs.

"Let's go." Amelia's voice rose shrilly. "Get the car, Grace. Get the car."

Grace put her arm about Amelia's shoulder. Amelia's body quivered like waves stirred by a rising wind. "It's okay, Amelia. They'll have the fire out in no time, I'm sure."

The Craines' and Herrills' homes and barns were ablaze. Numb and bewildered, the families huddled outside of Cove Road Church with their neighbors the Lunds, the Tates, and Pastor Johnson on the other side of the road. Heat assailed their arms and faces. Acrid smoke stung their eyes as they watched firemen from Madison and Buncombe counties fight a desperate and losing battle to save their homes. On the hills behind the houses arrowheads of flame marked the tree line where helicopters had dumped their vital cargo of fire retardants.

At the ladies' farmhouse everyone was now dressed. Hannah had brought black plastic trash bags upstairs. These she now distributed, one to each of them. "I expect they'll have this fire under control long before it reaches our house, but we can't stay here—the smell of smoke and charred wood will be suffocating. We'll go to Loring Valley and use our children's apartment. Put whatever you think you'll need for a few days, maybe a week, into these bags."

Hiccuping and crying, frantic to flee yet terrified to be alone, Amelia attempted to follow instructions. Frenetically she dumped everything on top of her dressing table—brush, comb, cosmetics—into the black plastic bag, and then every pair of shoes she owned.

Hannah and Grace tossed clothing into their bags, and Hannah, ever practical, emptied the file under her desk of papers: the deed to the property, their tax records, wills, birth certificates, and other documents. No one thought of taking Amelia's photographs or antique fan collection, or Grace's treasured clowns or collection of treasured cookbooks, or Hannah's gardening tools and books. Finally, clutching their bags, they stood in the hall.

"Go on down, put your bags in my station wagon—it's last in line. We'll be right down," Hannah said.

Across from the ladies, at George (Max) Maxwell's dairy farm, a congregation of cows, darkly etched against the orange glare, were being herded high onto the hills behind the barns. Men with hoses pelted Maxwell's lawn, windmill, house, and barns with torrents of water. As the vehicles passed his property, Max broke from among the firefighters and ran across the road to the ladies, who stood as if frozen on their porch.

"God, Hannah." He grasped her. "They're evacuating everyone. Damn. I thought they'd have it under control by now. Are you all right?"

Terror reigned in Amelia's eyes, numb bewilderment in Grace's. Unwittingly, Hannah slumped against Max for a moment. The relief in her eyes was transitory, and turned to despair. After tossing their bags into Hannah's wagon, Max shepherded them across the road to his lawn, then raced back to move the station wagon from their driveway. Shortly after he rejoined them, they stared in disbelief as fire trucks trampled Hannah's rosebushes, as more lengths of hose were unfurled, as great bursts of water struck their home and showered down windowpanes.

Grace broke from them and dashed back to their farmhouse. "I'm going after our things!"

Amelia's pupils dilated with fear. "No!" she screamed. "Grace, no!"

Hannah raced after Grace.

Dashing past firefighters, Max snatched the women about their waists and struggled to pull them back. With amazing strength, Grace broke loose. Max raced after her, Hannah following across the lawn, up the slippery steps, and into the farmhouse. The wood floors inside were slick. The rug in the foyer and the carpeted stairs oozed water. A caustic layer of smoke hunkered about them.

Grace was already upstairs, coughing. In the hallway, smoke darkened the space.

Steps thudded on the stairs. A fireman yelled, "You people crazy? Out of here. Out. Now!"

Max yanked Grace's arm. "You heard him. Let's go."

Hannah called to Grace. "Come on. Hurry."

"I want my clown that Bob gave me," Grace called back

"No time." Max held the towel to his mouth and coughed.

Wayne Reynolds, a close friend and volunteer fireman, was beside her. "Outta here, Miss Grace. Back of your house is burning." His strong arms wrested her out onto the lawn and thrust her, stumbling and coughing, toward Hannah, who shuddered when she saw the greenhouse she had sold to Wayne already consumed by flames.

Grace heard a man say, "This house is gone, too." Under the yellow parka, his eyes were red and his tired face damp. A long dark smudge ran down his cheek. He pointed to the ladies' farmhouse just as a paramedic ran up to Grace with an oxygen mask and tank. She held the mask tight and breathed, short gasping breaths and then more deeply.

"Let's get them outta here!" the paramedic shouted to Max above the din as he pressed them away from the house.

Moments later they stood in front of Max's house and watched with horror as flames danced triumphantly on the roof of the farmhouse they had so lovingly renovated and moved into three years ago. Thick gray smoke billowed from its windows and poured from every nook and cranny of the old homestead. Firefighters staggered back.

A young fireman dashed up and demanded, in no uncertain terms, that they leave Cove Road.

"Go to Bob's place!" Maxwell yelled above the din.

Hannah nodded. Four dispirited women, one nearly hysterical, climbed into Hannah's old station wagon and drove toward Elk Road.

AT HOME IN COVINGTON

The Diary

Hannah squeezed a finger beneath the folds of the thick brown wrapping paper, worked it open, tore it away, and lifted the lid of the box inside. A sealed envelope with unfamiliar, slanted handwriting lay atop a small leather book. Something inside Hannah tightened. Her throat constricted, and for a moment she looked about her with misgiving, as if she feared being apprehended and berated by the book's owner. Then, overcoming her presentiment of trouble, she extracted a letter from the envelope and unfolded it.

Hannah Parrish,
My name is Alice Britton Millet. I am the granddaughter of Dan and Marion Britton. I am forwarding this diary, which belonged to my grandmother. I believe that you are the Hannah Parrish referred to inside. If not, I apologize for sending this and ask you to please dispose of this diary and my letter. I feel I must tell you how I came upon this diary, and why I sent it. My grandfather was killed in a boating accident many years ago. If you are the Hannah referred to in its pages, you will know this. My grandmother remained in their home. She never remarried, and a year ago she passed away. It fell to my sister, Jane, and me to help our mother go through the

house in preparation for selling it. This diary was found in my grandmother's dresser drawer. My mother knew nothing about you. She was shocked and cried for days. When she threw the diary in the trash, I retrieved it and set about trying to locate Hannah Parrish, to whom I thought its contents might be meaningful. My husband is a private detective, and based on information in the diary, his investigation led me to you. And so, with trepidation, and against the wishes of my sister, I am sending it, wildly, unreasoningly, as one would send a note in a bottle.

Alice Britton Millet

The idea of being investigated, of having her private life scrutinized by a stranger, angered Hannah. She lifted the diary from its nest in the box as one would lift an injured bird, gingerly, and held it between the palms of her hands. She had loved Dan Britton too much and for too long. His death had been a misery, sundering her heart into a million pieces, and now the memory tore at the mended places. Uneasily, she opened the cover. The first entry read:

Dan is in love, but not with me. I know, because I asked him point-blank and he confessed. Her name is Hannah Parrish, such an old-fashioned name, and Dan wants a divorce. The Church won't let him do it. He says he's going to ask the Pope for a dispensation. I laugh at him. Our children and grandchildren belie a plea of non-consummation of our marriage, though for years we've slept in separate rooms. I would never agree to a divorce. I prefer to live without sex, without love, rather than suffer humiliation in front of the community, my friends, my family.

Dan had told his wife about her, had asked for a divorce. It had been Hannah's impossible dream. Her heart leaped in her chest, and the next moment her stomach tightened and grew queasy. The next entry in the dairy was dated many days later.

I saw that woman today. She works for a chiropractor. She's tall, not nearly as pretty as I am. She's quite angular, really. What can he possibly see in her? I'm still beautiful, people say, and I've kept my figure. Men still look at me when I walk into a room. Dan says I flirt, and why not? I get little enough attention at home.

The diary slipped from Hannah's grasp onto the flagstone walk. She covered her hot cheeks with her hands. Dan's wife had seen her, knew who she was. Had Marion seen Hannah in the street, at the bank? Had she come into the office? Hannah felt violated. One nudge with the toe of her shoe would send the little brown book tumbling into the water, its writing doomed to blur, its pages to dissolve among the curry-colored koi and the matted roots of lilies in the canal. She extended her foot, then hesitated. The diary had provided an answer to the old tormenting question of whether Dan had really loved her. He had. He had wanted a divorce, would have fought for a divorce. Why hadn't he told her? She thought she knew. He was a cautious, thoughtful man who made no promises to her that he could not keep.

The pain of loss reasserted itself and speared her heart. She thought of Max, his kindness, his reliability, his availability. "Oh, God, no," she muttered. "I hardened my heart back then. I can't bear to love anyone that way again." Hannah bent and retrieved the diary. Placing it in the box, she secured the wrappings and rose from the bench as she tucked it under her arm. Then she strode through the archway. She wanted to get home to show the diary to Grace.

A COVINGTON CHRISTMAS

Grace Singleton turned down the road to the church, where she had agreed to help young Pastor Denny Ledbetter clean out the church's attic.

As she climbed the narrow pull-down stairs, Grace heard Denny Ledbetter's alarmed voice.

"Good heavens. This is impossible! It's just terrible!"

"What's impossible?" she asked, sticking her head into the dim attic.

Pervaded by a musty odor, the attic was a dank, dusty room without ventilation other than the slatted ovals embedded in opposite walls. Two bare bulbs crusted with dust dangled on ancient wires from the ceiling. Denny sat cross-legged in the middle of the room, fenced by boxes.

"This." He held out a folder and waved it in her direction. "Most of this stuff is disposable, mainly bank statements dating from the late 1970s and 1980s. But then I found this. It's shocking and unbelievable. Come, read it. You won't believe it. It's very upsetting." He pulled several deeply creased letters from the folder and handed them to her. "Mrs. Singleton, if what this letter says is true, it's explosive."

"Call me Grace, please. Everyone does."

Grateful that she had remembered to slip them into the pocket of her jacket, Grace pulled out her reading glasses. Dated December 1, 1963, the letter was written on fine parchment yellowed with age, and addressed to Griffen Anson, Chairman of the Cove Road Community Church Council, Covington, North Carolina. The content was startling, and brief, and Grace read aloud.

Dear Mr. Anson,

We regret to inform you that Richard W. Simms has not been granted a degree from the seminary, and therefore the presbytery, which recommended Mr. Simms for seminary training, will not allow his ordination. Mr. Simms is thus not authorized to perform baptisms, weddings, or other rites and ceremonies, or to conduct services or to be deemed a pastor. Many fine young men have been graduated, and we would be pleased to assist you in your search for a pastor for your congregation.

Sincerely yours,
John P. Garner, President
McLeod Theological Seminary in Ohio

Attached with a rusted staple was a copy of another letter from the presbytery executive, confirming the fact that without a seminary degree Simms could not be ordained. Neither letter contained an explanation as to why Simms had failed to graduate.

"What is a presbytery executive?" Grace asked.

"Simms must have been a Presbyterian, and this letter is from the churchman who was overseeing his training and ordination. Something quite serious must have happened for them to dismiss him and not ordain him."

Denny shuffled several documents. "There's more. These are unsigned marriage certificates for the Craines, the Herrills, and three couples named McCorkle. Simms married them all between October and November of 1963. The church called him to service and installed him before they got these letters, I guess, and dear Lord, Simms never filed these marriages with the court." His eyes widened. "You know what this means, Grace?"

"I'm not sure."

Denny smoothed the yellowed papers on the top of a box. "The couples Simms married were never really married, and he knew that.

And whoever this Anson was, he knew it, too, and apparently chose to say nothing about it." Denny stared at the far wall as he tapped the letters with his fingers. "I'm sure Pastor Johnson has never seen these. He told me that he'd never bothered with anything in the attic."

Aghast, Grace stared at him. "This means that Frank and Alma Craine, Velma and Charlie Herrill, are not married?"

"They must have gotten licenses and blood tests. But these certificates are supposed to represent legal proof of their marriages by a bona fide minister, and they were never recorded. The couples whom Simms married were not then, and are not now, married in the eyes of a church, or even legally at the courthouse."

"What will you do?" Grace asked. "These couples have lived all these years thinking that they're married. Will you throw the certificates and the letters away, or will you tell them about this? And Pastor Johnson?"

"He's not well; I don't want to upset him. And I can't begin to imagine the trouble this would cause if it became public knowledge. I need to think about this. I'll pray on it for a few days."

"Surely they're considered married under common law," Grace said hopefully. "Many states recognize such marriages. What would be the point of telling these five couples now, after all these years?"

"I'm not sure North Carolina is a common-law state. I'll have to check that out."

They descended the unsteady stairs, and Denny shoved the stairwell up into the ceiling with a thud.

TWO DAYS AFTER THE WEDDING

"Miranda!" Hannah laid her wedding dress on the bed and embraced her daughter. "Come in. I'm so glad you made it in time. I would have hated getting married without you being here."

"A storm grounded the planes in Philadelphia last night and we were stuck until way past midnight. But here we are! How are you? Are you nervous?" She held Hannah by the shoulders. "You look marvelous. I'm so happy for you and Max. Who would have imagined you getting married?"

Hannah lifted the dress from the bed. "How does this dress smell to you? I've been airing it. It's new, but it's been in plastic for a long time."

Miranda brought the dress to her face. "Smells fine to me, like roses. It's a lovely dress. I didn't figure you for the white, flowing gown type; this is just right."

Satisfied, Hannah hung the dress on the closet door. "Go on down and chat with Amelia while I finish getting ready. Have you seen Laura yet?"

"Not yet, we're meeting at the church. I'll go ahead now so Laura and I can chat a bit before the ceremony starts.

With Miranda gone, Hannah scrutinized herself in the mirror. If I were only shorter and not so square shouldered. If only I were delicate, more feminine, like Laura or Amelia. With the palms of her hands she pulled the skin of her cheeks taut. Her wrinkles vanished. She removed her hands and they reappeared. Amelia had offered to camouflage those wrinkles with makeup, but Hannah had declined.

Why was I so stubborn? Maybe I didn't really believe this wedding would take place, or that Pastor Johnson would be up to the task. I like Denny, but I want Pastor Johnson to perform the ceremony. Lord, I am fretting. I worry that I'll start down the aisle wrong foot first, and be out of step with Amelia and Grace, or they'll start before the wedding march, before I begin to move, or Melissa will freeze with fright, and I'll fall over her. Will people giggle when I walk in with Amelia and Grace on either side of me rather than Bob, or Hank, or even Grace's son, Roger? Stop already! You'll make yourself crazy.

Hannah tipped her head to one side. If I get much grayer, I'll be white-haired. A hat would cover that, but I refused to wear a hat. Frustrated with herself, Hannah turned away from the mirror. Oh, where was Grace? She needed her support and help to get ready.

Rain pelted the roof of the farmhouse like thousands of tiny pebbles. Water streamed along both sides of Cove Road.

"I'm so nervous, Grace. Do you think this rain is a bad omen?" Hannah asked, as Grace adjusted the lapels of her wedding dress.

"Goodness, no. Weather is weather, always unpredictable. So don't start working yourself up about ill omens. You're going to get to the church and walk down that aisle, and everything is going to be absolutely perfect."

Hannah turned worried eyes to Grace. "Don't say perfect. Nothing is perfect."

"All right, everything's going to be fine. Is that better?"

Hannah nodded.

"Hannah, you look lovely."

"You really think I look okay, Grace? You wouldn't lie to me, would you? I feel like an idiot."

"You look regal, like a queen. Just stop wringing that handkerchief into a knot." Grace checked the time. "We have to go now, Hannah."

• • •

As she moved with Grace into the vestibule of the church, Hannah could hear soft music issuing from behind the closed doors of the sanctuary.

Dressed in pale green organza and standing quietly before her mother, Melissa held a basket filled with pink rose petals. Emily also held a basket brimming with petals. Her eyes bright as fireflies on a dark night, Melissa smiled up at Hannah, and Hannah knew there would be no misbehaving.

Amelia advanced toward them with Lurina wearing her lavender dress with her new hat tipped to one side in a jaunty fashion. For an instant, Hannah panicked. She should have bought a hat! Then Lurina smiled at her and patted her hand, and Lurina's touch and the tenderness in her eyes rendered Hannah less anxious, less eager to turn and run.

Then Amelia reached up and placed a crown of fresh flowers on Hannah's head. Standing on tiptoe, she kissed Hannah's cheek. "You look beautiful."

Hannah's heart filled with affection for her.

Mike handed her a bouquet of lilies and roses. "Break a leg, Hannah, darling."

Hannah clutched the flowers, her hands shaking. Then a rush of cold air heralded the opening of the front door. Max, elegant in his dark blue suit, entered with Tyler and Lucy, who were dressed perfectly for the occasion: Tyler in a light blue suit; Lucy in a pale blue, ankle-length dress with a bow at the waist.

Tears blurred Hannah's eyes. He looks wonderful, so handsome. Is this really happening to me, after all these years? Everybody came—the church is totally full. Good God, help me get through this. Why did I agree to this? It's silly, walking down an aisle like a girl of twenty.

But it was all happening. The music trembled and stopped, and the wedding march began. Suddenly Hannah stood in the open doorway of the sanctuary. Grace and Amelia offered their arms, and Hannah slipped hers into theirs. Together, they walked gracefully down the aisle in perfect sync with the music, and as they did, Hannah's anxieties melted away. She simply walked toward Max, unaware of the filled pews, of neighbors and friends, of her grandsons, her daughters and their husbands, of her foreman, Tom, and Anna and Jose, and all the others whose bright eyes and happy faces were turned expectantly toward her.

Hannah saw only Max. His eyes were fixed on hers, drawing her to him. She forgot their ages, forgot how silly she thought this was. It wasn't silly at all. It was glorious! Her heart was the heart of a young woman, her joy the joy of a young woman, her love was the love of a young woman for a young man.

Later, Hannah could not recall the pastor's words, or even when they said, "I do." She did remember feeling proud and happy, and the feel of Max's strong arm as he led her back down the aisle. She would never forget the bright smiling faces looking at them, wishing them well. She had walked on a sea of rose petals, and thought one word: "Perfect."

THE THREE MRS. PARKERS

In the Beginning

The tall, silver-haired woman appeared calm, her face composed. Only the tremor in her hand as she clutched the handle of the Amtrak train's door betrayed the strain of the journey and her agitation.

The porter set her two brown suitcases on the wooden platform, then flexed his fingers, making the joints pop. "Mighty heavy, lady. Whatcha carryin' in there, stones?"

Winifred Parker stiffened. She now regretted refusing her daughter-in-law's offer to pick her up, telling Zoe she was perfectly capable of getting there by herself. But the ride from Goose Island to Portland, Maine, followed by the long train trip to Philadelphia, and then Amtrak's East-West Express to Westminster, South Carolina, had sapped her physically.

The porter stood immobile, waiting for a tip.

"Call me a taxi, young man."

"I ain't got no phone." He lifted his hands in a helpless gesture and shrugged. "Gotta get you inside for that, lady."

Extracting her change purse from her deep leather pocketbook, Winifred counted out a dollar in quarters. The porter scowled, pocketed the money, shook his head, turned on his heel and moved away, abandoning her with bags too heavy for her to handle. Already she regretted coming.

• • •

Zoe Parker stared through the bow window over her sink.

It was silly, frivolous, and perhaps inappropriate for a fifty-two-year-old woman, but it lightened Zoe's heart, on warm nights when the moon was full, to slip into a white cotton shift, descend the steps, and cross the bridge to the summerhouse. From there the lights gamboled on the surface of the pond, and Zoe would lie in the hammock, relax, and release her mind to conjure up Steven, his red hair burnished by moonbeams. As in her memories of their too-short marriage, he would extend his hand to her, and they would dance. These moments brought the realization that she was perhaps too much alone, even though she worked with a local theater group and was helping to write a grant proposal to fund the renovation of an old theater, a home for their amateur company. It was a change from her usual work for environmental causes, but she'd needed a change, and she enjoyed working with the artistic director and the company's manager.

The kitchen phone jolted Zoe from her reverie.

Thick fog lay across long stretches of Highway 11, and Zoe held her speed to thirty-five. They hardly spoke except about the weather. Winifred perched on the edge of her seat, one hand on the dashboard, and declared unequivocally that of all the places she had ever lived, the weather was the most predictable and pleasant in Philadelphia. Then silence, self-conscious and thick as the fog, settled over them.

Zoe's mind drifted back to when she was still Zoe Amorey, about to receive her master's degree in education.

Steven Parker's fire-red hair, long and wild about his square, honest face, and those amazingly intense green eyes had startled her when she looked up from a game of checkers at an off-campus pub. He had stood to her right, his eyes warm and seductive. In that moment, Zoe had lost both the game and her heart.

Their attraction had been immediate and their romance fiery, and when she started down the aisle—two months pregnant, to her mother's chagrin and his mother's horror—Zoe had glided on air.

After weeks of trying to prevent their marriage, Steven's parents had presented him an ultimatum: Zoe, or his law education and his place in his father's law firm. Steven chose Zoe, then enlisted in the air force and was stationed at Caswell Air Force Base in Fort Worth, Texas. There Kathryn was born with her father's hair and eyes, and Zoe embraced the role of wife and mother. Those had been the happiest years of her life. Then on a cloudless afternoon, as Zoe shaded her eyes from the glare of the setting sun, she saw Steven's plane become a speck on the horizon. The gusto, the intellect, the passion that was Steven Parker vanished on a routine training mission. And Zoe, after months of immobilizing depression, managed to pack their few belongings and returned with her two-year-old daughter to her parents' home in Greenville, South Carolina.

Zoe turned off the highway onto a dark, winding country road. When the house came into view, Winifred said, "My God, how can you tolerate living way out here?"

Zoe's stomach knotted. "I love it here." Already it was clear to her that their arrangement, negotiated by phone, would never work. Winifred Parker, imperious and willful, a woman of means, could never adjust to rural South Carolina, and Zoe dreaded losing her privacy. Her heart plummeted as she considered certain of her personal habits: a trail of shoes left here, there, and anywhere, the unwashed dishes piled in the sink all day, books and papers strewn haphazardly on tables, laundry lifted from the dryer and left unfolded. Every habit, every move she made, would be subject to the scrutiny of Winifred's censorious eyes.

Living with her mother-in-law, whom she had not seen or heard from in years, would be untenable. How could she have imagined otherwise? How could she share her home with a woman she disliked and who disliked her?

But so much was at stake. She'd lived through tough times before; she could again. She would swallow her pride, adjust, and adapt to her mother-in-law and the situation. After all, Winifred wouldn't be here very long.

"The house is very comfortable, and we have neighbors now. See those lights?" Zoe waved in the direction of the pasture and pond. In the distance, tiny lights played hide-and-seek among trees on the far hillside.

"Where?"

"Over there, on the hill across the river."

"What kind of people would move way out here?" The scorn in Winifred's voice was unmistakable.

"There are two retired couples and a family with children. Nice people."

Winifred ran trembling fingers along her strand of pearls. She had never trusted this unwanted daughter-in-law. In those first months after Steven died, she had expected every letter to contain a demand for money from his widow. None ever had. But for a very long time she had needed a scapegoat, someone it was safe to hate and to blame for the loss of her only child. She understood that now.

Winifred squinted into the darkness. The unending chatter of insects grated on her nerves. She dreaded the isolation, and worried about the distance from a hospital. Already she loathed the house on Amorey Lane. She loathed the whole area. *Damn life's capriciousness. Damn growing old.*